HELEN ROW TOEWS

A GARDEN
OF
Promises

VINCI
BOOKS

By Helen Row Toews

Chateau de Belliveau

One Golden Summer
A Garden of Promises
Moonlight Over the Cinque Terre
When Love Blooms in Paris
With Love From Paris

Vinci Books

vinci-books.com

Published by Vinci Books Ltd in 2025

1

A CIP catalogue record for this book is available from the British Library.

Paperback ISBN: 9781036702861

Chapter One

Elyse Belliveau tapped a nervous foot under the patio table. She should have retreated inside long ago, but the heavy umbrella over her head had provided shade from the blazing heat of the late August afternoon in Provence. Folding her hands, she leaned back into the cushions of her deck chair with a sigh. She'd been sitting in this exact spot for what felt like hours; staring alternately at the pages of Le Monde, the most widely read newspaper in France, and a glossy fashion magazine. It was impossible to concentrate on either. Her eyes swivelled to where her mobile phone sat beside her. She willed herself not to check it for the umpteenth time.

Lifting her gaze, she stared across the glassy surface of the pool. Later it would feel good to slip into the refreshing water and cool herself after another day of heat. But not now. Not when her thoughts were focused on her daughter-in-law, lying in a Marseille hospital bed.

She turned her attention to the well-tended gardens of Chateau de Belliveau. They always brought peace to her soul. Taking a deep breath, she allowed the delicate perfume of the late, ruby red roses situated nearby to flood her senses. Farther away, on her right, a vegetable and herb garden featuring large waving fronds of aromatic rosemary, clumps of lush green basil, and delicate sprigs of thyme, grew next to a high stone wall covered with the deep orange flowers of trumpet vines, and the riot of purple, pink, and white clematis. Beyond the pool, and down the center of the garden, bright fuchsia bougainvillea draped itself over three standing trellises, creating an arbour. It was beautiful.

A wide bench had been erected beneath the dazzling centerpiece. She loved to sit under its dappled shade, even on hot afternoons, but particularly during the cool of twilight. Paths, created from finely-ground, light-coloured gravel, wound through the rest of the garden. Their borders were hedged with dwarf boxwood. Cicadas buzzed in the oaks and pines that were scattered through the area along with one old olive tree and a line of cypress at the far end.

She breathed deeply, allowing the calm serenity of her location to soothe her worried mind. She would not succumb to fear just because she hadn't heard from Julien. It had only been twelve hours since he and Angelina had rushed away, and calling his mother would be the last thing on his mind. Still, she checked her phone again, peering at its blank face and willing it to ring. Dropping it back onto the table, she picked up the newspaper this time and forced herself to scan the front page. There was a lengthy article covering infrastructure improvements slated for the Port of Marseille, an unsolved murder on the streets of Nice, and the story of a well-known Parisian company implicated in fraud. She tried hard to focus on reading, but the words blurred.

Elyse almost fell out of her chair when the phone burst

into strident ringing. She snatched it up, fumbled, almost dropped it, and then lifted it to her ear with breathless anticipation, rising to her feet with excitement. The turquoise silk caftan she wore swirled around her sandaled feet.

"'Allo," she said in a croaky voice, tucking a lock of glossy chestnut hair behind her ear. Pressing the phone closer in an effort to hear as well as humanly possible, Elyse waited. She cleared her throat, swallowing the concern she'd held at bay since early this morning, and snatched a tissue from the nearby box. Poised and ready for the tears she knew would come, she listened intently. "Julien! I am so glad to 'ear from you. What 'as 'appened? Is Angelina alright?" She spoke in English just in case Angelina could hear the conversation, then paused again, plugging the opposite ear with her fingers so she wouldn't miss a word.

"*Oui*, I can 'ear you," she cried after long moments. "*Félicitations!* I am so 'appy." She sank onto the chair with weakened limbs. "I understand. Kiss them for me, *s'il te plait.*" Dabbing at her brimming eyes, Elyse felt as though her heart would burst.

A slight movement caught her eye. Armand Dubois, the Belliveau family's personal chef, poked his head through the open French doors, looking anxious. She waved him over, a grin stretching across her face as she finished the call.

"My love to you all. *A demain mon cher.*" She tapped her phone to hang up, spun it across the table, and flopped back with a sigh of relief. Especially during times of great emotion, it was difficult to remember she should speak in English for Angelina's sake, although the young woman's French was improving every day. Elyse rounded on her friend, barely able to contain her excitement. Armand had been with the family for many years and had seen them through some difficult times. He was more than the family's chef. He was her dear friend, and she knew he loved the Belliveau family as a whole.

"The baby was born half an hour ago. It is a little girl." With a sob of happiness, she stood shakily to her feet and lifted her arms to him.

Armand obliged. His strong hands swept around her waist, lifting her from the tiles, and twirling her around the patio. She grasped his shoulders and her sun hat lifted. Before she could reach for it, the wide-brimmed *chapeau* flew to the tiles. Elyse giggled.

"This is wonderful news," he exclaimed, setting her down, but not relinquishing his hold.

She threw her arms around his neck and laughed, kissing his cheeks four times in an exuberant *bisous*. They were behaving like two teenagers for goodness' sake. She should show more decorum. Stepping back, she disengaged herself and hurried to pick up her hat before it blew into the pool. The only other time Armand had hugged her was after her husband had passed away in a car crash. That had been over a year ago, and the embrace was offered as a gesture of support—kind and caring. This time was different, and she felt a moment of strangeness, but Elyse shook it off. Happiness bubbled in her heart.

He beamed. "What is the baby's name? Have they decided?"

Elyse raised hands to her flushed cheeks. "Oh...I—I forgot to ask," she said. "I was so glad Angelina was well and the baby healthy, that I didn't think of it." She sank onto the chair and dabbed at her eyes with the tissue. "Thirty-one is so much older than I was when I 'ad my first child. Of course, women have children much later in life now, and I didn't want to worry them, but…" she admitted and shrugged. "I was concerned for Angelina."

"Of course, you were." Armand pulled out the chair beside her and sat down. "Because you are a good person. A thoughtful, loving woman who, once again, will make a fine grand-mère." He reached for her hand and twined his fingers around hers, squeezing lightly. "I have never known anyone I respected more."

Elyse stared at him. He had never said anything quite so personal, or complimentary to her before. Yet, it was not entirely unexpected. Lately, she had begun to feel a change in their relationship. Armand had always been professional, even aloof at times. But for the last few months she'd caught a certain look in his eyes as they rested on her face and a tenderness in his voice when he spoke only to her.

He wore his usual pristine, white chef's jacket and grey, pressed pants that almost exactly reflected the colours in his hair and neatly trimmed moustache. His hair was short, receding a little these days, but longer on top causing it to stand straight up. Despite the delicious food he cooked, he still remained slim and fit for a man nearing sixty. He was handsome, there was no doubt. Yet Elyse was not interested in relationships now, or perhaps ever. Armand was her friend, nothing more, and that was how she wanted to keep it.

She pulled her hand free, ostensibly to push her shoulder-length, bobbed hair away from her face. She then straightened as she fidgeted with the box of tissues, keeping her eyes downcast. Armand bent across the table toward her.

"There might be a better time to speak to you, Elyse… but my heart, filled with happiness for you and your family, will not allow me to be silent any longer."

5

She furrowed her brow and leaned away. *No. Not now please.* Elyse groaned deep within. She didn't want anything to mar this day.

"Armand, you…"

He shushed her by laying a finger across his lips. "I need to say this, *ma chère.*" Armand took a deep breath and sought her eyes. "I—I care for you a great deal. I will not say how much. You are a remarkable woman; strong, brave, and…" he paused, "so beautiful. I know you have been through a great deal, and perhaps you are not ready to hear this, but…I adore you." He clasped and unclasped his hands several times, almost hesitating as to whether he should continue. Yet his gaze didn't waver. "I do not expect declarations of love in return. I only ask that—that you could look beyond my lower station in life and give me hope that maybe—someday—you would consider accompanying me on—on a date."

Expressions of shock and dismay must have reflected in her eyes, because Armand had stumbled through much of what he said. He leaned away, hope mingling with concern in the expression on his face. Elyse was at a loss for words. Part of her had known this was coming, but none of her wanted to face it. Particularly not today.

"I don't know how to respond…Armand." Lightly, she touched his arm and then pulled quickly away. "I do not wish to hurt you, but I have not thought of anyone in that way…other than my husband Georges, for many years. I'm not sure I ever will." She took a breath and looked across the garden that she loved. "It 'as nothing whatsoever to do with you or anyone's 'station in life' as you said. I respect the man you are and what you do. I…" She stopped and he scraped his chair back abruptly, lunging to his feet before she could finish.

"Of course." He smiled down at her, his lips stretching into a frozen position. He waved a dismissive hand with forced nonchalance. "It was foolish of me to disrupt your excellent news with my own thoughts and feelings. There is no need for you to explain further. I will begin preparing the evening meal and then I believe I shall retire to my rooms for the day. Tomorrow, you said the 'appy family will arrive?"

She nodded mutely. "*Bien*,' he nodded once and turned away. "Forgive me—Elyse." There was something very final in the way he said her name. As though a heavy door had just slammed shut between them.

"Armand..." Elyse called after his retreating figure. But he was already gone. "Oh Armand," she murmured, holding a hand to her mouth. "I am so sorry."

Chapter Two

Elyse threw open the front door and darted onto the outside landing. She'd been waiting impatiently for the slam of a car door, signifying the arrival of Julien, Angelina, and the new baby. She'd taken pains with her appearance today; straightening her hair and adding a slight upward flip at the bottom, applying careful makeup, and wearing a white silk blouse tucked into wide-leg fuchsia pants. Although she had forced herself to stick to her usual morning routine, her nerves were on high alert.

Julien grinned at his mother as he made his way around the front of the car and opened the passenger door. With great tenderness, he helped his wife from the vehicle, then turned his attention to the back seat of the Lexus. Angelina leaned on the car door for support, smiling joyfully up the creamy stone staircase to Elyse.

"Bienvenue à la maison mes amours," Elyse trilled, hurrying down to greet her beloved *belle-fille*. She slipped her arms around the younger woman's waist and squeezed gently,

remembering to speak in English. "I am so 'appy you are okay. *C'est dur*? It was an 'ard labour?"

"*Merci maman.*" Angelina hugged her back. "*C'est dur,*" she agreed huskily over Elyse's shoulder. "But worth every moment."

They stood back to watch as Julien carefully unstrapped the baby carrier from the safety harness. Excitement grew in Elyse. She blinked away tears, lifting her face to the ever-present clear blue sky of Provence in a silent prayer of thanks for her family. The newest Belliveau member was about to be welcomed home. She was overjoyed. Her only wish was that her dear husband could have been present, but Elyse was sure he was watching over them from above.

Julien straightened, looking somewhat harried as he slung the quilted, mauve diaper bag over his head. After pushing it to his back, he devoted himself to the tiny bundle of humanity in his arms. His hair stood at right-angles from his head, two days' worth of stubble darkened his face, and his navy button-up shirt, as well as his jeans, were wrinkled. Nonetheless, he looked proud and incredibly happy. That was what mattered. Elyse was glad to see it. She covered the distance between them in two strides.

He bent, tilting the sleeping child so his mother could see her sweet face. Elyse cooed as she lifted the minute hand and was rewarded when the tiny fingers curled around her pinky. The cherub was peaceful in sleep, long dark eyelashes spreading like little fans across her rosy cheeks.

Awkwardly, Julien hugged his mother with his free arm. When she stepped back, he then slid it protectively around Angelina's shoulders as she moved to stand beside him and fuss with the blanket that held their daughter.

"It is good to be 'ome," he exclaimed, kissing his wife. Angelina raised a loving hand to his cheek, her braid of

9

long, dark hair falling forward over her drawn, but contented face. She flipped it over the shoulder of her pale blue tracksuit. Her outfit looked loose and comfortable, perfect for her suddenly slimmer figure. She was missing her trademark red lipstick, but motherhood had beautified her face beyond compare. Elyse felt as though her heart might burst with pride for her growing family.

"You look pale, *ma cherie*," Elyse observed, peering closer at Angelina. "Let's get you inside where you can sit down." She took the young woman's arm and with slow footsteps they ascended the stairs. Julien followed them with the baby.

Closing the heavy door behind the trio, Elyse hurried along the hall after them as they made their way to the sitting room. Julien dropped the diaper bag and sank onto the sofa beside his wife who had lowered herself with a sigh and leaned back against the soft brown leather. Cradling the tiny bundle close, he pressed a kiss on her dark curls and then passed her to his wife. He watched them with adoring eyes as Angelina pulled the blanket away, smoothing wisps of stray hair. Elyse sat opposite, enjoying the demonstration of pure love.

A door slammed elsewhere in the house, and footsteps could be heard rushing toward them. Raphaël, Elyse's younger son, rounded the corner as he too came to meet the newest member of the Belliveau family. Julien leaped to his feet and strode across the room to greet him.

"*Félicitations!*" Raphaël cried. He embraced his brother with a laugh and kissed him soundly on each cheek. Then, he wheeled around and saw the baby was sleeping. He placed a finger to his lips and tiptoed closer to admire his new niece, leaning down to kiss Angelina in the same manner. "Does she 'ave a name?" he whispered.

"Celeste Ava Belliveau," Angelina said. Her eyes glowed

as she gazed at her tiny daughter. "Named after Julien's Grandmother, Ava Belliveau."

"*C'est beau*! That is so thoughtful of you to include your grandmother," Elyse said, clapping her hands approvingly. "She and Georges would be so pleased."

"Congratulations to you both," Raphaël said with genuine happiness. "I think you must be the happiest and best-looking family I know. Of course…" he caught himself up short and raised his eyebrows, "our sister Lia's family are also *tres beau*."

"*Bien sûr*." Julien inclined his head in acknowledgement. "*Merci*. But for me, Celeste is the most beautiful baby alive." He laughed unapologetically and seated himself again. "Did the business run smoothly in my absence?"

Raphaël laughed. "Did you think it would fall apart without you there, brother? It's only been two days. Of course, everything is fine." He shrugged and moved to sit beside his mother. Elyse sensed a shift in his mood. The glow left his face. He leaned forward, reaching behind his back for one of the burnt orange accent pillows. Pulling it loose, he fussed with it; examining the pattern as though he'd never laid eyes on it before. In this way, he kept his expression hidden when he asked Angelina a pointed question. "And 'ave you told your family back 'ome the good news?"

"Everyone," she answered, covering a yawn. "Sarah said to say hello to you all."

Elyse stole a furtive glance at her youngest son. It was easy to see he was trying to appear nonchalant with his vague question concerning Angelina's family back in Canada. But in fact, he still hoped for news of the flighty Sarah who had stolen his heart when visiting the chateau last summer.

"Where is Armand?" Angelina asked, craning her neck to investigate the hall. "He was so excited for the baby to arrive, I thought he would be here to greet us."

Elyse turned to look out the window as she felt colour steal up her cheeks. Cringing inside, she thought of snatching the pillow from Raphaël and using it to cover her own discomfort. In truth, she hadn't seen Armand since their discussion by the pool. She hadn't gone looking for him either, feeling uncomfortable with how things had ended. He had prepared the evening meal and left. A note, addressed to her, had been left on the table in the expansive kitchen. It had explained why he was leaving and would miss this special day.

"I believe 'e was asked to 'elp at the restaurant of 'is friend, Marguerite. I guess she's not feeling too well. Armand was not 'ere last night and I 'ave not seen 'im today, but 'e asked me to convey 'is love for you all and regrets that 'e could not be 'ere." Elyse shrugged and strove to change the subject. "Could I get either of you a drink? Some orange juice for the new mother, per'aps?" She smiled at Angelina, knowing by the frown that creased the young woman's forehead, and the quick narrowing of her eyes, that Elyse's explanation had not been accepted.

However, Angelina schooled her features and asked nothing more. "Not for me, thank you," she said. "I feel positively water-logged after all I drank this morning. I thought 'eating and drinking for two ended after childbirth. Turns out I was wrong." Angelina shared a knowing chuckle with her mother-in-law.

"I'm sorry Armand had to leave, though," Angelina continued. "I mean, I'm glad he's become close with his old friend at the restaurant, and is able to help her out, but I know how much he had wanted to see Celeste." She leaned against the heavy rolled arm of the sofa and kicked off her shoes. "I'm exhausted."

Instantly solicitous, Julien spoke in lowered tones. "Why don't you lie down for a while? When Celeste is hungry, I will bring 'er to you."

"You're sure?" Angelina raised her eyebrows, twisting around to search his face "You were up most of the last two days as well."

"My job was not quite so strenuous as yours," he answered dryly. Celeste was asleep against his chest. "We'll be fine. My brother will keep me company." Raphaël nodded in acknowledgement.

"*Merci, mon trésor.*" Angelina pushed herself upright with a groan. "Will you walk with me, Elyse?"

"*Bien sûr.*" Elyse stepped across the room. Anxious as she was to hold her new granddaughter, she knew there would be plenty of time for it later. That was the beauty of having her family take up their married lives here at the chateau.

"See you later," Angelina said to both men. Leaning over her husband, Angelina pressed a kiss onto his forehead and lifted a gentle hand to caress their baby's head before she caught Elyse's arm and together, they paced out of the room. As they mounted the broad curving staircase, Angelina asked the question that Elyse knew had been on her mind.

"So, what's really going on? I know very well Armand's intention was to be here today when we got home. Did something happen?"

Elyse laughed. "You are too smart for me, young lady." Yet, the smile died on her lips as she recalled the scene on the patio with her friend. She patted the strong, capable hand that rested on her arm and wondered how much she should divulge to her daughter-in-law. She took a deep breath.

"He's in love with you, isn't he?" Angelina said in a low voice. Coming to an abrupt halt, Elyse whirled around to look at her in disbelief.

"You know about it? 'Ow?"

Angelina grinned. "I saw the signs." She wound her arm tighter and tugged Elyse into taking another step. "It's in all the special little things he does when you're not looking, the way his eyes linger on your face, how his voice changes when he talks to you, or about you to others." She paused at the top of the stairs. "But you don't feel the same way, do you? Did you tell him? Is that why he isn't here?"

"*Mon dieu!*" Elyse reached out to steady herself on the railing. "How could you possibly know all this when I was so unaware? It is uncanny." She shook her head in amazement.

"No," Angelina said with a rueful smile. "It's an inherited trait. If I so much as breathe funny, even over the phone, my mother knows something's wrong and already has half an idea what it is before I can summon the wherewithal to deny it." She giggled. "It's an amazing talent. Maybe motherhood brings it on," she noted and flung an all-encompassing arm wide. "I do know how annoying it can be to others though…so, I'm sorry." She looked at Elyse with dancing eyes.

They reached the top of the stairs and turned to walk along the hall toward the left wing of the house, and the large suite of rooms that Angelina now shared with Julien. Sunlight streamed through the long, latticed windows that graced the landing on either side. Though thanks to central air conditioning, the chateau was cool and comfortable.

"I don't know 'ow I missed it," Elyse rubbed her temple

and frowned. "I feel terrible about 'urting 'im, but you are right. I don't feel the same as 'e does, and it would not do either of us any good to pretend otherwise." She stopped at Angelina's door. "I thought 'e was dating 'is friend Marguerite. Didn't you?"

"For a time, I did. But I believe she is truly just a friend." They stopped outside the door to Angelina's apartment. She pulled her mother-in-law close and held her tight. "It will all get sorted out in the wash, as my mom always says. Don't worry. If that's how you truly feel, it was best to tell him."

Elyse made a conscious effort to smooth her brow, and hugged Angelina back. "I am so very glad you married my son," she said, holding Angelina's arms and pulling away to look lovingly at the girl. "Now, try to 'ave a nap before Celeste insists on the return of 'er mother." She opened the door and gently pushed Angelina through. With a tired wave Angelina closed it behind her. Elyse retraced her steps, sinking into deep contemplation.

Memories of her beloved Georges crept into her mind. She felt as if she was betraying him with all this nonsense. Although it had almost been a year and a half since he died. She shook her head to rid herself of those thoughts and marched back downstairs to spend time with Julien and his beautiful little daughter. She simply couldn't think of romance. Not now and perhaps not ever.

Chapter Three

Elyse leaned on the black marble kitchen countertop the following morning. She stared out the kitchen window, sipping her second *café au lait*. When would she next see or speak to Armand? The note hadn't mentioned when he'd return. He hadn't been back to the chateau since yesterday when they'd talked by the pool. She was starting to worry he wouldn't return. But that was crazy, wasn't it? She knew seeing him again would be awkward, but they were friends. Good friends. Surely this situation could be worked through.

She blew the hair from her eyes and stared pensively out the window, pondering all he had said. The sentiments he professed to have for her couldn't be real. The two of them would talk, clear the air, and go back to the easy friendship of before. She straightened, telling herself it would be okay. After all, she didn't want to lose him.

A leafy Boston fern graced the broad windowsill, the leaves a rich green in the morning sun. She ran her finger-tips through the fronds and breathed in the rich aroma of her coffee as she cradled the cup in her free hand and gazed at her garden. It always cheered her, usually.

Clarisse was vacuuming in the dining room. The loud hum of the machine was grating on her nerves, and soon she would arrive to clean the kitchen. Elyse pushed away from the counter with a sigh. She must prepare for the day.

"*Salut*," Armand said at her elbow. Startled, she swung around, nearly spilling her drink. Reaching out, his fingers brushed hers as he took her cup and placed it on the counter. He unhooked a large black bag from the crook of his arm and let it drop to the floor.

"Armand. I didn't hear you come in. Good morning." She smiled, but it quickly faded as she took in his serious face. In fact, he was wearing jeans and an orange t-shirt instead of his usual chef's garb. While the colour looked good on him, accenting the golden tan of his skin, it was unusual for him to wear casual clothes to work. "What is it? You don't look like yourself, *mon ami*."

He shook his head and ran a hand through his spiky hair. Clearing his throat as though about to deliver a rehearsed speech, he began. "I must tell you I have decided to take a position elsewhere. Unfortunately, the chef of a well-respected restaurant in Marseille has died and his nephew is searching for someone to take over until they can find a permanent replacement. He called last night to ask if I would accept the position as chef."

Elyse was stunned. She felt for the countertop behind her, never taking her eyes from Armand's. "You can't be serious," she managed after a long moment. Her face grew warm as she argued the point. "I know there is not much for you to do here, but we are starting to entertain more...and that will only increase as time goes by. The family is grow-ing, after all. Perhaps Raphaël will find someone to share his

life with and there will be more people and babies and…"
She was babbling and stopped herself.

Her breath caught in her throat as his features softened into a smile that nearly broke her heart. His eyes caressed her face as though committing it to memory. She knew why he wanted to leave. More than anything she wished she could tell him what he wanted to hear, so that he would stay. But it was not possible. Yet, he was like a member of the family and the thought of losing him pained her more than she cared to admit.

Armand spread his hands in an apologetic manner. "It has nothing to do with how busy I am. The slower pace of life here at the estate was enjoyable after a lifetime of rushing to serve the elite of Paris. My career's never meant as much to me as the people I love and…" he paused, took Elyse's hand in his own and lifted it to his mouth. She took a deep breath as his lips lightly brushed across her knuckles. His deep blue eyes darkened as they locked on hers.

"And I find that you and your family have become very important to me," he continued. "Too important, I suppose, because I cannot stay here without wanting to show you how much." Abruptly he dropped her hand and stepped back. "It is best that I go." His voice became business-like and correct. "I have arranged for someone to take my place. Marie Laurent will take care of your meals until you can find someone permanent. Of course, I will be back to arrange for the event we planned to welcome the new baby next Saturday. I would not want to miss that." He ran his hands down the front of his jeans as though they were sweaty and took another step back. "I have a very special meal organized, so I must be here to prepare and cook it." He glanced around as though seeking escape. "I should leave."

"Now?" she asked tremulously. If she didn't sit down soon, she was going to fall. Somehow, she shuffled to the table and dropped into a chair.

"Yes. My clothes are packed, and my rooms have been tidied. I will gather my knives and a few essentials to take with me, the rest can be secured later. You will likely see me each day this week as I cannot take everything all at once." With a sigh, he bent to pick up the bag, and moved to the kitchen island where he pulled out a drawer. Rummaging inside, he drew out a long black case and fitted it inside the bag along with a few other utensils. Then he went down on one knee to tug out a large frying pan from beneath. Straightening, he closed the drawer and leaned heavily on the counter, avoiding her eyes. "I believe this is for the best..." For a moment, he stared out the window where he had worked for the past six years, then, turning, he walked quickly to a door that led into the garden and pushed it open.

Blinking rapidly, Elyse rose to her feet and opened her mouth to say something more, anything really. Except her insides were churning, and her heart caught in her throat. Something precious had just come to an end. She had to stop him before he left, but words failed her. What could she say? Nothing he wanted to hear. Armand looked back briefly and lifted a hand of farewell before he disappeared through the door.

It was a somber crew that met for the evening meal that night. Elyse made the announcement over a tureen of delectable leek and potato soup that Armand had left chilling in the fridge. Both Angelina and Julien had accepted the news of his leaving without comment. She gathered from the meaningful look that passed between them that Armand must have spoken with her son privately. What he had said to Julien, she didn't know, nor did she want to know.

Of course, Raphaël would need to be informed. He was busy attending a meeting with a few local olive oil producers in the city and wouldn't be back until late. She would ask Julien to speak to him then. Elyse didn't want to make the painful announcement twice. Lia, Elyse's daughter, wouldn't be affected by the news, since she and her family lived in Marseille. Lia would be sad that Armand was leaving, but she could be told at another time.

Elyse was grateful that further explanations weren't necessary. After a few moments of awkward silence, the evening was redeemed by the happiness only a new baby can bring to a home.

The three of them retired to the spacious sitting room, talking over a minor breakdown of some machinery being readied for the imminent harvest. Angelina stifled a yawn as she sank into the pillowy-soft sofa with Celeste cradled in her arms. Julien walked to the heavy wooden bar at one end of the room to pour a glass of *vin rosé* for himself and his mother, and a fresh orange juice for Angelina which was her preference while nursing the baby. He delivered their drinks as they settled down to enjoy the cool air conditioning after another hot day.

The room hadn't changed much in twenty years, Elyse thought, remembering a time when she and Georges had reclined on the heavy leather furniture. The sun would stay high in the sky for at least another hour, so the ornate lamps placed on bulky wooden end tables about the room were unnecessary. She and Georges had picked the furniture out several years before his death and she loved its solid comfort even now. Elyse stared into the beautiful cream-coloured stone fireplace that roared with bright orange flames during the winter months, but for the time being stood empty. Perhaps it was the arrival of a new life, but she found herself once again feeling grateful for her home and family. The only thing missing was Armand, padding silently in from the kitchen to visit with them. She shook herself and straightened. No, he had gone, and it was for the best. She might as well get used to it.

Celeste lay peacefully in her mother's arms, wide awake and staring at them with an alert expression as though committing each face to memory. She'd slept soundly her first night home which was a blessing. Elyse smiled as she looked across at mother and baby. Celeste appeared to be a content baby with zero digestive upsets, thus far, and a bright-eyed interest in her surroundings.

"Honestly," Angelina said, looking up with surprise, "I thought babies were supposed to cry all night and parents were always drained and run ragged from walking to soothe a wailing child." She caught a tiny waving foot and lifted it to her lips. "Celeste is a perfect angel."

"I can say with certainty that she didn't get that from your 'usband," Elyse noted with a smile for her handsome, sandy-haired son.

He rubbed the shadow of a beard on his jaw and looked pained. "Just what are you saying, Mother? That I wasn't the model child you've always led me to believe?"

She laughed. "This is not the time for unpleasant details. We'll leave that subject alone…for now," she said, wagging a finger at him and laughing. "Anyway, suffice it to say your father wore out a rocking chair and I did my share of pacing the floors, and not only when you were an infant.

Do you recall the botany club and my prize orchids? Oh, and does the name 'Enri Ricard mean anything to you?"

Julien joined in her laughter. "You're right. Best to leave specifics in the past where they belong," he said, shaking his head ruefully. "Some stories don't deserve a retelling."

"Are you kidding me?' Angelina said, her eyes alight with interest. "I have to know. You can't leave me wondering."

Julien settled back on the sofa beside her and crossed his legs, looking at his mother. "You should tell her the escapade with the botany club and I'll…" he lifted a hand and extended thumb and forefinger to indicate a small measurement, "Well, I'll tell her *un petit peu* about 'Enri."

Elyse took a sip of her wine and then set the glass on the end table beside her before folding her hands and looking off into space. "Julien was always a precocious child. 'E was inquisitive and active; we never knew what 'e would do next. When 'e was about nine years old, Julien developed a fascination with insects." She waved a hand to illustrate. "We found cicadas chirping in the curtains, butterflies fluttering against the dining room windows, and beetles crawling in his bed. 'E was stung by wasps more times than I can remember." She turned her gaze upon her oldest child and smiled. He smirked back.

"I cannot deny it," he said, shrugging one broad shoulder.

"At this time, I belonged to a botany club," Elyse continued. "I 'ave always loved plants. I was very interested in orchids and 'ad been cultivating three special varieties that were very close to blooming. The temperature and 'umidity must be just so, *tu comprends*?" She leaned forward to look at Angelina, clasped her hands, and leaned her elbows on her knees as she warmed to her subject.

Angelina nodded.

"I was anxious to take pictures of the blooms for my next club meeting and forbade the children to even enter the greenhouse where the orchids were kept. In 'indsight, I should 'ave set the plants in trays filled with rocks and a little water to achieve the tropical atmosphere they required. But instead, I chose to mist them. One day I grabbed my bottle and began a liberal application. The leaves were beaded with moisture, and I hummed a happy tune until the odor of chlorine filled the air." She shook an accusing finger at her son who playfully hoisted a cushion and used it to shield the dark looks his mother shot him as she relived the event all over again.

Julien took over the retelling. "*Ma pauvre mère*," he said, chuckling as he shook his head sorrowfully and stuffed the pillow behind his back. "I 'ad borrowed the bottle and filled it with bleach in order to kill ants on the sidewalk."

"*Oui!*" Elyse said. She swivelled to direct her question to Angelina. "Can you believe it? This man, who today, would not even kill a fly. I was so angry with 'im—"

Angelina's eyes widened as she gazed at her husband in mock horror.

"In my defense," he interrupted, holding up his hands, "the ants were unlawfully entering the kitchen. You complained about them yourself, *ma mère*."

"It's true." Elyse said, sinking back into the sofa and reaching for her wine. "And I paid dearly for those unwise remarks concerning those annoying insects. My plants shrivelled up and died on the spot."

"Oh no." Angelina giggled. "That's a great story though." The baby waved her chubby little arms and gurgled as Angelina shifted her into a more comfortable position. She looked pointedly at Julien. "Next story?" she prodded.

"I was 'oping you would forget," he said with a sigh.

"Not a chance."

Watching her son squirm at his wife's insistence, Elyse laughed again.

He began with a disclaimer. "I was only a boy, so don't judge me too harshly. *D'accord?*" Angelina kissed the baby's forehead and nodded, winking at Elyse.

"*Mon ami*, 'Enri, and I, spent the summer we turned sixteen on our motorbikes touring the countryside. One day, we stopped near Nimes at *une fête de village*. You know that is a village festival, correct?" He paused, waiting for her nod of understanding. "In any case, we were mesmerized by the *Course Camarguaise*. My parents had only taken me to one as a small child and, as older boys, we found it fascinating. After that, we visited every *fête* we could find and eventually got the idea to—"

Angelina interrupted. "What is that? The course Cama-who?"

"Bullfighting," Elyse said, rolling her eyes. She heard Angelina's sharp intake of breath and hastened to explain. "Don't worry, *ma chère fille*. It isn't the same as you might see in Spain. The bull, or the cow in some cases, is never killed or even 'urt. It is strictly a show that takes place in the southwest, the Camargue region of France. The animals are bred especially for this purpose, and they lead a good life. They only fight six or seven times a year, retire at fourteen or fifteen, and then are put out to pasture until they die a natural death. The animals are buried in an upright position with their 'eads facing the sea." She shrugged. "It is all quite dignified. If anyone is injured it is often the foolish young men who get into the ring with them."

"Okay," Angelina said doubtfully. "Tell me more." She hesitated, looking down at Celeste cooing on her lap. "It might be best of you never repeat this tale in front of our daughter, because I have a feeling it isn't going to end well."

"It's not going to end at all if you don't let me finish," Julien retorted with a smile. "And just so you're aware, no animals or people were harmed during the course of these events." She opened her mouth to say something more, but he held up a hand and continued to speak.

"Now, as I was saying, one summer, 'Enri and I went to quite a few afternoon shows and got the idea that we would become famous bullfighters. All we needed was an opportunity. We'd been studying the techniques of some talented *razeteurs*. Before you ask," he said, dipping his head and raising his index finger, "that's one of the names for the young men who fight." He glanced at his watch. "It's getting late. Don't you think…"

"No, I don't," said his wife. "You're not getting out of this. Continue."

Julien twirled the glass in his large hands. "Bien. We decided to go see the large evening spectacle in a village twenty minutes away, against our parents' wishes. Then, we pretended to be bullfighters from Arles, so we could 'ave a chance to get in the ring." Julien looked embarrassed and stopped to gulp the remainder of his wine. "'Enri stayed 'ere with me that day and some'ow we snuck out of the 'ouse and rode our bikes there without anyone knowing."

Ducking his head, he looked at Elyse and grinned. "It was foolish, I know. When we arrived, we found that a square pool 'ad been constructed at the center of *la place de la ville*. The town square," he amended. "Truckloads of sand 'ad been brought in, and huge lights lit the scene. There were stands full of people, hundreds of them, all waiting

25

impatiently for the festivities to begin. Most of them 'eld plastic cups brimming with wine or *pastis*. The sky 'ad darkened to a deep blue over'ead and the moon rose. It was all quite exhilarating for a couple of young boys."

"I'm sure it was," his wife said dryly. "Get to the part where you were almost killed, please, because I feel certain it's coming."

"Would anyone care for another drink," he said, further delaying the culmination of the tale by lifting his empty glass with a sheepish grin.

"No!" Angelina said, answering for both her and Elyse. Celeste continued squirming happily on her lap.

Julien sighed. "Very well. 'Enri and I were shocked to see the pool of water. That 'ad not been part of any *Course Camarguaise* we 'ad been to before and we didn't know what to make of it. On top of that, the officials, for some unknown reason, 'ad allowed us to participate, and we were the first ones called into the ring. We 'ad no idea what to do. Thankfully, the announcer explained the objective of the first event to the crowd. We listened carefully and not without fear. After all, we 'ad never taunted a charging bull before. It was much different to be in an enclosed space with the infuriated beast than it was to simply watch from the stands."

Elyse sighed, reliving the fear she had experienced when the strident tones of a telephone had woken her that fateful night.

Angelina stiffened, waiting for the climax of events. "I'm afraid to ask, but what was the goal of the first game?" she said.

"Thankfully, there were two other young men who joined us, or we would 'ave made complete fools of ourselves, since we didn't understand what was going on."

Julien shook his head ruefully. "After all, we were invited to join the games only by lying." He rubbed his hands across his knees. "The objective was to tease the bull into charging us and ultimately to 'ave him leap into the pool after us."

"I assume the beast had horns…" Angelina asked in wide-eyed wonder. "Aren't people gored?"

Again, Elyse answered. "The tips of the horns are usually blunted, so they cannot do much harm if they come in contact with a person. Still, with an animal that large and powerful, damage can be inflicted." She gave her classic shrug. "It is the risk these young men are willing to take for the thrill of the sport and the admiration of the crowds."

"I learned afterward," said Julien, "that the whole objective was to lure the bull into the water by running just a few steps a'ead of it. Then you were meant to leap onto the edge of the fabricated pool, and drop into the water close to the edge. So, the animal would lunge overtop and you would not be trampled." He sighed again and leaned forward to clasp his hands. "'Enri and I were not aware of that last bit of critical information."

"And…?" Angelina prompted when he lapsed into silence once more.

"Oh…I tried to sprint through knee-deep water in front of a fast, remarkably agile, infuriated beast weighing around 500 kg." He shook his head. "It didn't go so well."

"Julien!" Angelina squeaked in fear. "What happened?"

"The bull caught my clothes with 'is horns partway across the pool, threw me into the air. I landed in the sand on the other side, with the air knocked out of me, 'e picked me up and tossed me again. Fortunately, at that point the other *razeteurs* came to my rescue and enticed 'im away while I was 'elped to safety."

"That was when the authorities learned Julien's real

name," interjected Elyse. "They called Georges and me to come get 'im…at the 'ospital."

"The hospital?" Angelina closed her eyes to take a deep cleansing breath.

"*Oui*," finished Elyse. "We were sick with worry as we raced there. That escapade cost 'im two broken ribs and a fractured tibia from landing on 'is one leg at an awkward angle."

"It marked the end of my summer, and my bull-fighting career," Julien added with a dramatic flourish of his arms. "I spent the next five months recovering. Ultimately, I decided to stick with grapes and olives as my livelihood. At least they don't fight back." He attempted a little laugh.

Angelina leaned back and surveyed her husband through narrowed eyes. "You could have been killed."

"I am well aware of that. It is not a story I am proud to tell, but you did ask." He stood and stretched, sticking his leg out in front of him and doing circles with his foot. "No lingering effects," he remarked with a chuckle. "Now, one last drink and then per'aps we should retire." He collected their glasses and moved to the bar.

Angelina reached out to catch his hand as he passed, and a loving look passed between them.

"I am so glad you were okay, my love," she said. "Thank you for sharing your story. We all do foolish things when we are young. It comes with the territory." She gazed down at the now sleeping Celeste. "Even our daughter will get into mischief, I am sure."

"That's 'ard to believe. Celeste is such a dear, sweet baby," noted Elyse with a smile. She lapsed into her own thoughts as her eyes followed the movements of her oldest son and felt a surge of pride in her heart. Marriage had only changed him for the better. Before meeting Angelina, he had become rather embittered toward women and life in general, but now...he was a loving father and husband.

She thought of her own marriage to Georges. They had enjoyed thirty-seven years of happiness before his untimely death in the car accident. He hadn't even told her of the cancer he was fighting at the time, lest it worry her. She plucked at a loose thread on the armrest. Theirs had been the perfect relationship. She didn't see how there could be anything more for her in this life and would be content with her memories.

Elyse swallowed a lump in her throat as Julien bent solicitously over his wife to kiss her before handing over the glass of juice he had just squeezed. Julien took after his father in every way, and it did her heart good to witness it.

"*Merci*," she said, as he stepped to her next with the tray of drinks. She accepted the chilled glass of rosé, closing her eyes and allowing herself to imagine that Georges sat beside her on the sofa.

Lost in her thoughts, she was surprised when a knock sounded at the massive oaken doors in the foyer outside the salon. Julien leapt to his sandaled feet, hurried through the arched doorway, and disappeared. They were all dressed very casually this evening. Today had been hotter than usual, and everyone wore their coolest clothes. Julien was dressed in a loose, pale blue t-shirt that hung over his tan shorts. Hastily, he tucked it in as he exited the room.

"Were you expecting visitors?" Angelina straightened, her long, loose-fitting, crimson dress rustling around her body as she transferred a sleeping Celeste to her shoulder and began to rub the infant's back.

"No." Elyse craned her neck to see who had arrived. She glanced down at her own clothing. Her old jean capris she kept for gardening and a sleeveless green cotton blouse wasn't company attire. Who could it be? All of their friends knew Julien and Angelina had just brought home their baby, so it couldn't be any of them. Was it an emergency of some sort?

A jovial male voice could be heard in the hall. It didn't sound like anyone she knew. She considered avoiding them by ducking out the back door that led to the kitchen on one end and down a few steps to the wine cellar on the other. But she was too late.

As Julien rounded the corner with another man in tow, she thought she recognized him as the American man who had spent time with them the previous year. He'd spent almost a month in the Provence area last October and had visited Chateau de Belliveau each evening to speak with Julien about buying olive oil wholesale. She had assumed their business could be conducted from afar this time around, as was the way of most overseas companies. None of the other buyers she knew had time to visit each press, every year. How unusual that the man should return.

"Bonjour Madame Belliveau," he said, rushing to Elyse with a hand extended. "I don't know if you remember me. My name is Edward Wright, but please call me Eddie. All my friends do." He was a slim, muscular fellow, probably six feet tall with thinning blond hair. His nose was slightly off center as though he'd been a boxer in some past life, and he wore wire framed glasses that continually slid down his nose. While this made him look slightly bookish, Elyse knew that an active curiosity and bright mind lurked behind those spectacles. He had a warm, engaging smile and light blue eyes that sparkled with pleasure as they met Elyse's own. His brown suit was tailored and hung from his shoulders with elegance, despite being a trifle rumpled. He set a small leather case down with a thump and grasped her hand, wringing it up and down as though his life depended on it.

She was glad to see him, but the force of his enthusiasm took her off guard. Colouring, she backed away with a simple friendly greeting and sank into the sofa once more.

"And I hear that congratulations are in order for the newlyweds," he gushed. "Oh, what a sweet little mite she is, too. A proper little princess, that's what." He advanced upon Angelina with purpose in his stride. Elyse met her daughter-in-law's wide-eyed look of shock over Edward's shoulder as he patted the baby's pink, lacy bottom in her cute little, short set. Then he whirled around to march across the space and plunk himself down beside Elyse.

"Sorry if I've been too forward with y'all," he said, speaking to what Elyse imagined they were all thinking. "It's been a hard day, and it means a lot to see a friendly face." He sighed and peered at each one in turn. Taking a deep, peremptory breath, he dropped a bombshell. "I was robbed at the airport in Paris this afternoon. Didn't even know it was happenin'. They took my wallet, credit cards, driver's license, and worst of all, my passport." He shook his head sorrowfully as the family erupted with concern.

Julien punched an angry fist into his hand. "Unbelievable! Did you speak to the authorities? What did they say?"

"I'm so sorry to hear this," cried Angelina. Celeste awoke with a whimper and Angelina rose to pace the floor with the baby in her arms. "Is there anything we can do to help?"

"Oh la la," Elyse moaned. "You will never get those things back! They are too skilled, these pickpockets. 'Ave you called to cancel your credit cards?"

"The police were sympathetic and helpful as far as lettin' me use their phone at the station, but they said I'd never get anythin' back. I cancelled it all. I'll need to contact my embassy tomorrow about a passport," he said, nodding first at Julien and then Elyse.

"Fortunately, I had my cell phone, plane ticket, and thirty euros in another pocket." He shrugged. "So, I flew here, grabbed a sandwich at the airport, and took a cab to your front door. I hope you don't mind a visit. I can't even drive without my licence, and I sure can't pay for a hotel, or food for that matter," he said, tapping his chin thoughtfully.

"You must stay with us," Julien said with a decisive nod. "Paris is a large city filled with tourists who sometimes are disoriented or completely unaware of thieves in their midst. It is a sad fact that visitors to our country are often preyed upon by unscrupulous people. I am so sorry you were robbed, but you are among friends now. We will see you are well taken care of." He moved to clap Edward on the shoulder in reassurance. "I will speak to Clarisse immediately and have 'er prepare a room."

Elyse murmured her agreement as Celeste broke into full-on crying.

"Please excuse me," Angelina raised her voice over the wails of the hungry baby. "It's after eight, so I think we'll retire for the night." She flipped her ponytail over her shoulder and hoisted Celeste higher, the tiers of her voluminous red dress swishing around her legs. "Good night, Edward, you came to the right place."

"*Bonne nuit mes chères filles.*" Elyse stood to kiss her daughter-in-law and granddaughter as they walked from the room. Julien addressed his mother and Edward.

"I believe I will 'elp my wife with our baby," he said with an apologetic smile. "Do you mind showing our guest to 'is room, *ma mère*?" She nodded. "I am glad you felt you could come to us for assistance, Monsieur Wright. Please, try to get some rest and we will do what we can for you in the morning."

"Thank you kindly, Julien," Edward said, scrambling to his feet. "But please, call me Eddie." He nodded with appreciation at both Belliveaus. "I sure am thankful to know such fine people as yourselves."

Julien acknowledged this statement with a brief salute and then he was gone, taking the stairs two steps at a time as he endeavored to catch up with his family.

"Are you goin' to bed too?" Edward turned to Elyse who had walked to the long, polished wood bar at one end of the room. On her way she paused to draw the floor-to-ceiling brocade curtains, for privacy, and flipped on a lamp.

"Not yet," she smiled. "I thought you might enjoy a glass of wine where it's cool and restful. It 'as been warm and I am sure you've 'ad a stressful day. Would you like to sit and relax for a while?"

"I'd like that a lot." Edward took off his jacket with a grateful sigh and laid it on top of his case. He then accepted the chilled glass of *vin rosé* from Elyse and followed her lead, seating himself across from her on the sofa with a sigh of contentment.

"Julien will 'elp you in the morning," she said. "The robbery must 'ave been traumatic, but those things can be replaced, and you are safe 'ere with us...uh, Eddie."

He smiled as the unfamiliar name tumbled from her lips. "I'm real thankful to be here ma'am," he said. "I hope you never have to go through somethin' like that. It was a shock to the system for sure."

"Well, it's over now." Elyse sipped her wine. "You said you 'ad a plane ticket. Was it to Marseille?"

He nodded over the rim of his glass.

"I presume you must 'ave been coming to see Julien

concerning the olive oil, but 'e made no mention of your arrival." She looked at him enquiringly.

Eddie laughed. "The deal fell through last year," he said. "The company I represent had filled their quota of oil from Italy, Spain, Greece, and Portugal before I could present the information I'd gathered from your estate. It was unfortunate, but it won't happen again. That's why I wanted to get here early and earmark as much oil as you can sell." He shifted uncomfortably. "Reckon I should have contacted Julien to let him know I was comin'. Sorry about that ma'am. For sure I planned to call from Paris, but then…" His words trailed off into nothingness and he buried his nose in his glass of wine, appearing too shaken to continue.

"I understand," Elyse hastened to reassure him. The last thing she wanted to do was make him feel worse about the theft. Such a thing had never happened to her, but she'd heard of plenty of people who had been stranded in a big city after being robbed. The man was to be pitied, not inter-rogated. She felt sorry for him.

A chiming bell broke into their companionable silence, making her jump. Eddie mouthed 'sorry,' then leaned back, and reached into one pocket. He dragged out a small flip phone, and flicked it open to consult the interior. "Damn," he said quietly, snapping it shut and staring into space. His expression darkened as he ran a hand through his hair, lost in thought.

"…Do you need to contact family back home?" she asked, after a moment's hesitation. "Or your company? Please know you are welcome to use our house phone. I imagine it would be expensive to call the United States from France."

"No, no, bless your heart lil' lady," he exclaimed, turning his attention back to her with a start, almost as though he'd forgotten she was there. His handsome face broke into a warm smile. "Y'all are too kind. I contacted my workplace from Paris, but I was madder than a wet hen when I called. It took some time to explain the situation. Once they understood, it took no time at all before they extended my stay here and told me not to worry. 'There's more than one way to skin a cat,' so they say…" He paused. "As for family…well, I ain't married if that's what you mean. I have a daughter in New York. She ain't worried about me none. My girl has her own life and family to take care of. Truth be told, I haven't seen her in years."

Elyse felt confused and knew her face registered it. "A wet hen?" she repeated, feeling dazed. "And a skinned cat! What do these things 'ave to do with anything? *Quelle horreur!*"

Eddie erupted into laughter, slapping his knees and rocking back and forth in his seat before wiping his eyes and calming himself. "You have to forgive me, ma'am. I use a lot of colourful sayings from the south where I grew up. Tennessee to be exact. I'll admit, that one about the cat is inappropriate if you take it literally, but it ain't meant that way. It just means there is more than one way to go about achieving your goal. And, as for the hen…well, you'd have to see a wet hen to know how mad they get. And I was really mad."

Once it had been explained, Elyse joined in the laughter, feeling light-hearted and carefree to be giggling with this interesting man in the salon. Perhaps more than she had since Georges had died. She looked at Eddie as he lifted his glass for the last few drops of wine and smiled at her. He was a breath of fresh air.

Elyse considered how fascinating it was that life could change from one minute to the next. She'd enjoyed her chats with Eddie last year when he'd visited the estate to learn more about the olive oil business. She'd found his accent charming and his forthright manner and lack of pretense intriguing. Somewhere deep inside, she felt a tingle of excitement that he had returned.

Much later, while lying in bed, Elyse recalled that he'd said he hadn't seen his daughter in years. She'd been so focused on the absurdity of his descriptive phrases, that it hadn't registered. What sad situation had prompted such an unhappy separation? She would have to ask him once they knew one another better.

If she were honest, she was very much looking forward to getting to know Eddie. A large part of her couldn't help but wonder if it was fate.

Chapter Four

Elyse yawned and stretched in the king-size bed she'd shared with Georges. Opening her eyes just a crack she saw the sunlight already streaming through the nearby windows and the gauzy white curtains wafting into the room with the aid of a gentle breeze.

What time was it? She rolled onto her side and reached for the clock on the bedside table. Not yet eight. Good. She flopped over and stared at the ceiling. A lot had happened in the past two days, and she was glad she could retreat to her spacious private rooms to mull it over. The space was decorated just how she liked it and filled with memorabilia she had collected over the years. Items she'd brought back from family trips, photos of her children at various stages of growing up, and paintings she'd purchased from her favourite artists. There were also framed drawings her children had created with childish hands, and one that her niece, Annette, had painted in acrylics when only ten years old. One day, that girl would go somewhere with her art.

Elyse propped herself up on soft pillows and looked

about her. It was a plain room, by some people's standards, as Elyse wasn't fond of fuss and frills. When she'd first married Georges, the space had been dark, adorned with thick brown carpets, and gloomy brocade curtains in shades of deepening russet with tiny smidgeons of rose thrown in to lighten it.

Except that it didn't. An enormous, weighty wooden bed had squatted at the center of the space, slathered in chocolate-coloured pillows and draped with a woven bedspread that looked as though it belonged in the Dark Ages. Every item in the room had served to turn it into the most depressing, dark, and dismal room of the house.

Elyse remembered turning to her new husband in dismay and asking him if he was okay with her making a few changes to his ancestral home. He didn't mind at all, and told her with a kiss. So, Elyse had ordered the furniture to be removed, torn down the drapes, thrown open the shutters, and welcomed in the sunshine. That was thirty-seven years ago. Most of the furniture had changed since then, but the theme had remained the same. Bright, open, and spacious—it was filled with light and an uplifting atmosphere.

She threw her arm across the bed to where Georges had always slept and swivelled her head to stare at the untouched pillow. It had taken time for her to become accustomed to his absence. Often, she would wake in the night, having felt his presence in this room where they had shared such precious moments of both joy and sorrow. It might have only been her imagination, but still, it was a comfort.

Propping herself upright, Elyse crossed her arms over the coverlet and gazed about the room. It was a huge space, the last room at the south end of the chateau and had the advantage of floor-to-ceiling windows on two sides. They were broad, taking up most of the west side, rounded at the top and recessed into the wall leaving an alcove where she sometimes sat to read or to look outside during the winter when the mistral was howling around the corners of her home. An ornate chandelier hung overhead, offering a soft golden light to the room when shadows lurked outside, and a fireplace opposite the bed warmed her toes when winter's icy blast kept her indoors. The room also boasted an enormous walk-in closet and two hefty bureaus painted creamy white in a luxurious French provincial style.

The windows on the other side of the room led to a private balcony where she'd loved to sit in the twilight of an evening with her beloved. She and Georges had shared their thoughts on life, concerns about their children, mused over the day's events, and planned their future together all on that balcony. Two bistro chairs and a small round table were out there, just big enough to hold their wine and a flickering candle. It had been a closely guarded time they had shared each evening after the kids had gone to sleep. For months following his death, Elyse couldn't bring herself to open the broad French doors and step outside on the veranda, but now she could. Those memories were sweet and poignant.

Cozy armchairs flanked the alcove on either side and a small desk was pushed against the wall where Elyse kept her laptop computer and a small television. However, she seldom used either of those devices, preferring to be busy with the family business during the day, her garden, and spending time with her loved ones, friends, or reading in the evening. She closed her eyes and considered their unusual houseguest.

Eddie. Even his name brought a flickering smile to her lips. Last night she'd led the man, along with his battered brown case, to one of the guestrooms that was less feminine in décor. He'd thanked her profusely at the door. After telling her he was 'dog tired,' which she assumed was another interesting colloquialism he used, as opposed to a weariness only experienced by canines, she'd left him to make himself at home and get some rest. She knew jetlag must have taken a toll on the man. Despite his pronouncement of dog tiredness though, he hadn't looked particularly sleepy.

Elyse hoped he'd stay with them at least a week. Eddie was fun to have around and would take her mind off of Armand's departure. With that final thought, she swung her legs out of bed and rose to her feet. She padded to the window and pulled back the filmy curtain to grasp the door handle and stick her head outside. It would be another hot day, as expected for this time of year in Provence. She pulled in a deep breath of fresh air, noting the scent of pine and hearing the cicadas tuning up for another day of courtship. The raspy sound was barely noticeable to her most of the time, but this morning seemed especially loud. She closed the door against the heat.

Turning, she stepped inside her closet and gathered an outfit before taking a shower in her spacious bathroom. A hot day called for a loose-fitting dress, and she had a plethora of them in every shade and hue of the rainbow. Elyse loved colour. It fed her soul and made her happy. She knew people thought she was chic and polished. Even though she always took care with her appearance, she didn't see herself that way. Some colours or styles didn't suit her at all, yet she still loved wearing them.

Today she'd chosen a long, sleeveless, sea-green dress splashed liberally with brilliant pink hibiscus flowers. It swirled around her ankles as she swayed to and fro. She felt pretty. A pair of flat, strappy sandals in metallic gold, and several long strands of mingled chains and beads completed her ensemble. She dug her hairdryer out of a drawer and stood with a round brush, blow-drying her glossy, bobbed hair into its usual fullness. As she studied her reflection in the wide, gilded mirror over her dressing table she thought perhaps she looked a bit like an aging hippie from the 60s era in her flowing dress and long rattling necklaces. But did she care? Not at all. She had no one to impress and felt happy with her outfit.

She switched on the overhead light and sat down to begin a careful, light application of foundation, rouge, a dusting of eyeshadow, and mascara to accentuate her deep brown eyes. Finishing with a delicate pink lipstick to match the hibiscus, she pushed her chair back and smoothed her hands down her dress. Perfect. Now ready for the day, whatever it might bring. She smiled at herself and headed downstairs.

The house was quiet. Elyse passed through the dining room and entered the kitchen, feeling the need for an espresso rather than her regular *café au lait*. She paused to lean over the sink, staring into her treasured garden. As a rule, Armand would have already been outside, fussing with the herb beds or tending the flowers. He loved it as much as she did. They had spent many happy hours working together and chatting.

She shook her head. That was quite enough reminiscing. With practised hands she prepared her steaming drink, noting there were already two used cups in the sink. Once done she carried it to the table beneath the floating staircase that led to the rooms along the right wing of the chateau.

Julien rose early each morning and worked long hours in the vineyards and olive groves, so one cup must have been his. She could only assume Eddie had also joined him. She sipped her beverage, savouring the rich flavour with eyes closed.

A light tap at the garden door startled her. Elyse whirled around to see an older woman standing behind the glass, her grey hair scraped back and tightly knotted at the nape of her neck, with sharp brown eyes and heavy eyebrows set in an impassive face. She was solidly built and wore a knee-length white, almost clinical dress that buttoned down the front. It looked starched, as though when shed at the end of the day the garment might continue to stand in an upright position, propped against a wall in this woman's home. Even the lady's shoes were white. They were an old-style wedge, but were spotless, appearing crisp as if they'd also been starched and then whitewashed to achieve maximum cleanliness.

Was this the chef Armand had told her he would send? The person meant to fill the gap his leaving had caused. Elyse sighed. You couldn't judge by a person's appearance, she knew, but even at first glance this lady was off-putting. She hurried to the door, her flowing skirt almost tripping her up as the fabric wound around her ankles.

"*Bonjour*," she said with a bright, and what she hoped was welcoming, smile. "*Puis-je vous aide, madame?*" And then, because it flashed across her mind that perhaps the woman wasn't French, she followed in English. "Can I 'elp you?"

The woman regarded Elyse without expression, dark eyes taking in the flamboyant outfit with an audible sniff of disapproval. She spoke in a voice not unlike tires crunching across a gravel road.

"*Bonjour. Je parle anglais et français,*" the woman continued in clipped French. "I am Marie Laurent. Your former chef, Armand Dubois, asked me to come with very short notice, a thing I detest, but he said you were desperate. And so, I am here."

"I don't think desperate is the right wor—" Elyse began, but Marie interrupted.

"Immaterial," she said sharply, waving her hands dismissively. "May I come in? I wish to see the kitchen facilities. Armand said they are adequate, but I would like to be sure. From there I will decide if I will stay, or not."

Elyse stepped back and Marie bustled inside, tossing a large handbag onto a chair, her sharp eyes raking over the room. Elyse was almost amused by the woman's high-handed approach. Marie Laurent would be the one to decide whether she would stay or not, would she?

The scene took on a feeling of incongruity. Elyse couldn't imagine Armand choosing this bulldozer of a lady to be his replacement. It was unbelievable. Elyse was still standing by the door when the woman finished her loop, having peered into cupboards, pulled out drawers, and tested the weight of many shining saucepans hanging above the workstation.

"*Tres bien*," she announced, stopping in front of Elyse and placing her hands on ample hips. "I will stay."

Again, Elyse was taken aback. Apparently, as the employer, she had no say in the matter. She bit back angry words, took a deep breath, and was just about to calmly tell this imperious woman to exit her home when Julien walked into the kitchen with Eddie close behind.

"Welcome," Julien said, spreading his arms wide and, Elyse knew for Eddie's sake, speaking perfect English. "I see that Armand's aunt 'as arrived. 'Ow nice to finally meet you, Madame Laurent. I am Julien Belliveau. Armand 'as told me so many wonderful stories of summers 'e spent with you and your family in Brittany. I almost feel as if I know you already." He grasped the lady by her shoulders and welcomed her with *les bisous*, a kiss on either cheek. Stepping back, he looked at Marie with obvious delight. "Thank you so much for coming. A room 'as been prepared for you upstairs."

Elyse's mouth fell open as the surly woman blushed and a sheepish smile spread across her face, wreathing it in lines. Marie's harsh exterior melted away like ice cubes on a summer sidewalk, and she raised a flustered hand to flatten her already perfectly smooth hair.

"You are most welcome," she said, her tone softening. She followed her host's lead, also lapsing into English. "It will be my pleasure to cook for your family until a suitable replacement can be found. I 'ave only one condition."

If Julien was surprised, he didn't show it, Elyse thought, as she watched this firecracker of a woman make demands upon her new employer.

"My *très jeune petite-fille*, Genevieve, was coming to stay with me for the summer and I could not turn 'er down after she looked forward to it all year. She will stay with me 'ere, *oui*?"

Julien's eyebrows lifted, but otherwise he was the picture of diplomacy and tact. "Certainly," he said. "Your grand-daughter is also welcome."

"*Bien!*" the lady said briskly. "She will arrive by train to Marseille Saint-Charles station in two days' time. Armand will pick 'er up and bring 'er to me. I must 'ave time to spend with 'er when she arrives. *N'est-ce pas*?"

"Certainly." Julien agreed without hesitation. "Please take all the time you need. It must be a long trip to make alone for someone so young." He looked beyond Marie, as though just noticing Elyse was in the room. "I see you met my mother, but I would like to introduce you to our guest, Edward Wright. He will be staying with us for a while."

"*Enchanté*," said Marie with a stiff inclination of her head.

"*Bonjour, Madame Laurent*. It is so nice to meet you" said Eddie, stepping forward and gravely bowing his head. "I look forward to sampling your food. I'm sure it will be as delicious as you are lovely."

It was blatant flattery. Elyse looked at the older woman to see what she would do with it. She fully expected her to call it for what it was and dismiss the man, but she didn't. Elyse was shocked to see the ironclad lady blush and coquettishly smile up at him. Madame Laurent was easily won over by a handsome face and a few sweet-talking words.

Elyse stared surreptitiously at Eddie as he went on to ask questions about the lady's journey that morning, what Brittany was like, and to tell her she didn't look old enough to have a granddaughter. Elyse rolled her eyes as the lady fluttered her eyelashes and beamed at the man.

Granted, Eddie was looking good today. If one were interested, which she was not. The patterned blue button-up shirt he wore strained over his broad shoulders and was tucked into the waistband of white linen trousers, accentuating his lithe form. He was clean shaven, and his fair hair lopped casually over one eye giving him a rakish air. The glasses lent him a studious look which added to a general appearance of sophistication.

Mon Dieu, she was in danger of fawning over the man herself. She tore her eyes away from him and over to their new cook who had turned to face Elyse, her jaw hardening into a forbidding line as the smile disappeared.

"I will prepare the evening meal if you can find something for yourselves at lunch?" She looked around at the three of them, sounding doubtful.

Julien had been watching the scene play out with a half-smile curving his mouth. *The rogue!* He was enjoying this. Elyse motioned to him that he should step forward.

"*Bien sûr Madame Laurent*. We are capable of a simple meal. I am sure you would like some time to accustom yourself with the 'ouse. I will be 'appy to 'elp you in whatever way I can."

"*Bien*," the plump little lady said. "Armand is bringing my cases from the car. I don't know what is keeping 'im. If you would excuse me, I will check."

Elyse moved to one side pulling the door wide and the shorter woman marched through the opening as though time was of the essence. Elyse held the door open for Marie's return.

Clearly, Marie didn't need to learn Elyse's name, since she hadn't asked for it. Just what had Armand told the dour little woman? That Elyse had crushed his spirit? Broken his heart? Driven him heartlessly into the wilderness to dry up and wither away? Elyse sighed.

Not only was Armand gone, but this unpleasant woman must be tolerated until she could find another chef. Why hadn't Armand listened when she'd assured him, she'd take over the kitchen? Elyse sighed yet again. It was a double blow as far as she could see. If she hadn't had the incentive to find someone to run the kitchen and cater the many dinner parties they had before, she certainly did now. She would write up an advert immediately.

"Did you 'ave breakfast?" she asked the men as they waited for Armand and his aunt to return. Glancing at the clock on the far wall she realized it was almost eleven, a bit late for such a meal. Still, she could always make them something quick. She just hoped it wouldn't be under the evil eye of Madame Marie Laurent.

"We ate in Marseille," Eddie cleared his throat and spoke for the first time. "Julien took me to the United States Embassy this morning. He dropped me at their doors before they were even open." He rubbed his hands with invisible soap, looking pleased. "I spoke to a consular officer, and he told me I not only needed a police report, which I had, but also some evidence of U.S. citizenship like a birth certificate, driver's license or even an expired passport. Since all of my identification was stolen, the application is on hold until I can provide the necessary documents."

He lifted his hands in a helpless gesture. "There ain't much else I can do. But it shouldn't take too long to get sorted out. My company is interested in gettin' me back on the road. They want me in Spain next week, and then Italy. They suggested I wait here until my passport and other documents have been restored, so that I can keep travellin'." He rubbed a hand across his clean-shaven cheek. "That don't mean I have to take advantage of you folks and your warm hospitality though. My company can pay for a hotel in the city."

"Nonsense," Julien said, smoothly interjecting before Elyse could respond. "We are 'appy for you to stay with us for as long as you need. Is that not right, ma mère?"

"Oui," Elyse answered with emphasis. "You are among friends and are very welcome."

"I sure appreciate it," Eddie said, nodding gratefully. "That means a lot to me."

Shadows loomed in the doorway, and everyone turned to see Armand trudging heavily down the path. He held two massive bags and dragged one more. They tipped precariously to one side as he struggled to shove everything through the door. His aunt followed, also with her arms full. Her gigantic pile of luggage led one to believe she was planning to live out her life at Chateau de Belliveau. Elyse grew irritated.

"*Salut*, Armand." Julien stepped forward, helping the chef to safely set down the bags. "I'm sure you remember Edward Wright. 'E visited us last year to learn more about the olive oil business for 'is company back in the United States."

The two men nodded. "*Oui, bonjour*," Armand said, and then turned his back to the man as he focused again on his aunt's cases. He did not look pleased. An uncomfortable silence fell over the room.

Julien looked at his watch. "I need to get back to work, and I'm sure Marie would like to get settled," Julien said, rolling up his shirtsleeves.

Marie clutched what appeared to be a rather moth-eaten carpet bag in one hand and rolled a large black suitcase in the other. An old sunhat had been rammed low over her eyes and she peered out from under it with grim formality.

"I did not bring much," she barked, stepping around her vast pile of cases. She dropped her carpet bag to the floor where it fell with a dull thump followed by the faint aroma of lavender. The black bag she stood upright and looked at each man in turn. "If someone would 'elp me carry these things to my room, I would like to unpack and change."

"Shall we show 'er together?" Julien said to his mother. "I asked Clarisse to prepare Armand's old suite. Then *ma mère*, maybe you would like to take the car and show Eddie a few of the sights. I doubt if he feels up to talking business today and I have a full schedule."

"Of course," Elyse smiled briefly at Eddie, then forced herself to maintain the expression as she spoke again. "I will show Marie to 'er room," she said with far more cordiality than she felt. "You will excuse us?" She looked questioningly at Eddie and Armand who had moved to stand stiffly at opposite ends of the room. She frowned, not understanding the instant animosity that appeared between them.

Eddie nodded eagerly from the doorway where he hovered, appearing anxious to leave. He looked like a boy who'd been offered a day off school. Actually, she'd been thinking much the same thing. She wasn't thrilled about spending quality time with Madame Marie, and it didn't help that Armand stared glumly out the window. The idea of an outing with the intelligent and attractive Eddie appealed to her.

"I'd love to do some sightseeing," she said.

Chapter Five

Eddie excused himself and hurried away after saying he'd be ready for their excursion in half an hour. Julien took the case Marie had been dragging plus the one Armand had pushed. Armand grasped the last of the large black bags. They hoisted them up, their eyes bulging from the weight. Julien looked at Marie over his shoulder.

"What do you have in here?" he expostulated. "Bricks?"

The lady smiled grimly. "You may leave that one downstairs, Monsieur Belliveau. It contains a few of my favourite pans and some good-quality utensils."

Julien's jaw dropped. "You brought your own?" he asked. "But we h—"

"*Oui, oui.*" Marie answered firmly, cutting him off. Her eyes narrowed as they rested on her new employer. She enunciated slowly as though dealing with someone of lesser intelligence. "I always travel with the necessities of life." Behind her, Armand shrugged and trudged past them on his way to the curved staircase in the hall.

Elyse smothered a giggle. The 'necessities?' She wasn't

acquainted with many chefs to know if this was standard practise. But just the idea of packing your suitcase to take a journey halfway across France and feeling the most important items to bring along were a set of cast iron frying pans and some sturdy flatware, was hilarious.

The three of them escorted Marie up to the rooms across the hall from Eddie. Marie poked her head inside the door and asked the men to place her luggage on the floor beside the bed. They did as she asked. Julien turned with a smile to say that he would see her later, but the stout little lady sweetly barred his way. Despite Julien's assertions that he needed to return to work, Marie demanded that he walk her back downstairs and remain while she asked him some pertinent questions.

"This information is important," she asserted with a toss of her head as they walked toward the staircase. "You cannot expect me to cook for you without a thorough understanding of the situation."

Julien mumbled his reply, following in the wake of this demanding woman and swivelling his head round to look beseechingly at his mother. Elyse winked at him. They descended the staircase side by side, Julien moving with barely concealed impatience. Yet he catered to the little woman's demands with good grace. Elyse and Armand followed, saying nothing. She would have liked to resume their easy friendship, but the circumstances had made it impossible.

Armand's eyes shifted to her. "You look beautiful, Elyse. That colour suits you."

"Thank you. I am surprised to see you here today. When do you start work at the restaurant?" She kept her eyes trained on the stairs.

"Tonight," he said. They had reached the bottom step

and Elyse, despite carefully watching her feet, became tangled in her voluminous dress and pitched forward. She would have fallen, had Armand's strong arms not scooped her up and righted her.

"Oh la la," she exclaimed. "Thank you, Armand. Apparently, I need lessons in how to walk while wearing a dress." She tried to make light of it, but in truth a current of electricity had run through her at his touch. *Don't be ridiculous*, she told herself. That had nothing to do with him. It was only the sudden jolt of falling that had caused it.

"No problem." Armand strode ahead of her, but then, just as swiftly he whirled around. "Take care of yourself," he said cryptically. "I care about you, *chérie*."

Elyse was taken aback, but smiled noncommittally. Armand hurried to catch up with his aunt and after a second so did she. Though she pondered his statement for long moments after.

Marie strutted in front, reaching the main floor where her shoes squeaked across the tiled floor and her stockinged legs swished beneath the stiff folds of her dress. Elyse couldn't help but be intrigued by this eccentric woman and she forgot about Armand's words.

Upon returning to the kitchen, and with great deliberation, Marie fished a large black notebook from her handbag and sucked on a pen thoughtfully.

Armand took this opportunity to kiss his aunt and wish them all a pleasant afternoon before he ducked out the kitchen door and disappeared along the path. Had his eyes lingered longer on Elyse than the others? She wasn't sure.

Marie grilled Julien on family allergies, food preferences, the availability of fresh ingredients, and what free time she would have. She wrote all of his answers down while Julien tapped his foot impatiently.

Luckily, Angelina had avoided this whole fiasco by staying in the apartment she shared with Julien at the far end of the chateau. Had she also known Marie was coming? Elyse squinted suspiciously at her son as he outlined several of his favorite dishes. Later, she would ask him why he hadn't thought to warn her of the dragon lady's arrival.

Eventually, Julien escaped, grinning at his mother over Marie's head as he whisked through the kitchen door. He then jogged down a path that wound through the garden toward the family business.

They were alone. Thinking of a word her daughter-in-law often used in situations like this, Elyse muttered, "Great." Then she plastered a smile on her face and showed Marie the wine cellar, the pantry, and encouraged her to feel at home during her stay.

The new chef grunted her thanks and told Elyse she would like to familiarise herself with her new domain... alone.

Freedom! Elyse ran upstairs to change into more appropriate clothes for the day's new agenda; a pair of lemon-yellow capris, a white, short-sleeved blouse, and her trainers. She grabbed her purse, a floppy hat, and the keys to her car before calling to Eddie and scooting out to her vehicle to wait for him. *Whew.* If this strained situation continued it just wouldn't work out to keep the woman. She'd sooner starve to death than have Armand's aunt ensconced in the Belliveau chateau, glaring at her in her own home.

All she could surmise was that Armand had, for some reason, divulged the true reason for his departure to his aunt, and the woman had then come to her own conclusions. Still, it didn't sound like something Armand would do. She trusted him with her life. He wasn't the sort of person who would malign her to anyone or divulge his personal problems in an offhand manner. Perhaps Marie was like this with everyone. She pushed those thoughts aside as Eddie appeared at the car door and eased himself into the passenger seat.

"Where are we goin'?" he asked, as she put the car in gear and pulled away from the chateau. "I'm lookin' forward to this."

Eddie stared at the neatly trimmed lawn and orderly trees that lined the road as Elyse's red Audi purred down the driveway. Elyse smoothly shifted gears and made good on their getaway. She glanced in the rear-view mirror, half expecting Madame Laurent's dark, disapproving scowl to be floating in the air behind her.

"I thought I'd take you to visit one of the lovely villages in Provence. I presume you 'aven't seen much of France, besides the inner workings of an olive oil estate?" She looked at him sideways and he shook his head.

"Well, if you 'ave one or two days to spend 'ere, I would like to show you some of the reasons Provence is such a popular tourist destination…at least in my estimation." She stopped at the entrance to the Belliveau Estate and looked both ways before venturing onto the main road. "We can't do all the sights in one day, of course, but we could take a few trips." She caught herself sounding hopeful and tried to tone it down. "I realize your intention is to work while you are 'ere, but…" Her voice trailed away in embarrassment. Eddie had said he wasn't married, and present troubles meant he was forced to postpone his work schedule, but that didn't mean he wanted to tour the countryside with her as his guide.

"I was fixin' to do a pile of things while I was in Europe," Eddie said with an airy wave of his hand. "The plan was to travel to Spain after this, check out a few olive groves and then fly to Italy. My boss wanted me to visit several of the farms we import from. A personal touch, you know?" He looked at her inquiringly and settled back in his seat. "But I can't think of anythin' I'd rather do than see some of the countryside with a beautiful woman. I wouldn't have a chance to do that otherwise, so maybe this is a blessin' in disguise." He smiled at her, his eyes crinkling at the corners and pushed up his glasses.

Elyse nodded, with some effort she turned her attention back to what she was doing. She was surprised by her reaction. It was just a smile and sweet words, but Eddie was a charismatic man. Relaxing, she found she was looking forward to this day too.

He focused on the scenery and left her to navigate the road. It was paved, but narrow. They twisted their way up through the chalky hills where olive trees and grape vines thrived, but precious little else grew. Overhead, the brilliant blue sky of Provence lent radiance to the land, the heat of the sun beating on the earth, baking it hard.

Elyse had only learned to drive five months ago, at the age of fifty-six. She'd started out slowly. Though with Angelina's tutelage it had been easier than she'd expected, despite never having driven before in her life. She and Georges had gone everywhere together, and driving hadn't felt necessary when she was younger. Suddenly, with his passing, she'd begun to feel stranded and a burden to those who had to ferry her where she wanted to go. It gave her a good feeling now to climb behind the wheel and confidently drive.

Her thoughts drifted back to today's journey. Since earning her licence, Elyse often went exploring on her own. She had begun to re-visit the picturesque villages and fabulous scenery she'd been raised in, all within a two-hour radius of the estate. She'd grown up in the tiny village of Menerbes, in the Luberon region of Provence and had met Georges as a girl of eighteen. Since marrying him, and losing her parents at a young age, she hadn't been back much. But now she'd gone on her own many times, even Angelina had joined her to visit several of these charming villages. Armand had accompanied her a few times too, but her sons had always been too busy with the estate.

Scrub brush and stunted pine trees sprang up where the rocks were less and tall brown grasses, long since dried from the blazing heat, stood starkly in clumps—a fire hazard if ever there was one. This time of year was dangerous. A careless cigarette, a spark from someone's match, or a lightning strike often set off a catastrophic fire. In a moment's time, fire could take out hectares of forest along with homes and livelihoods. People who lived in the south knew the dangers, but so many people visited Provence that didn't understand. Fires were almost impossible to prevent. Worst of all, sometimes a blaze was purposely set by arsonists.

They crossed a wide highway and continued along the quiet road that led through a small town.

"This village is called Lancon-Provence," Elyse said, breaking the silence. She had assumed, wrongly, that Eddie would keep up a non-stop chatter and was relieved to learn that wasn't the case. In fact, she was now struggling to fill the awkward hush. "It isn't on my list of destinations. But it is typical of the local architecture with its small squares and lovely stone houses. Do you come from a big city?" she asked.

Eddie pursed his lips, thinking. "Big enough," he said at length. "Nashville ain't no small potatoes, but it ain't the biggest city in the U.S. either."

"Small potatoes?" Elyse cast him another sidelong glance. She knew it had to be another one of his colloquialisms, but she couldn't figure out what garden vegetables had to do with the population of a city.

He made a great guffawing sound that caused her to jump. The car swerved over the center line before she saw that he was only laughing. "Sorry ma'am," he said. "I gotta start thinkin' before I speak in this neck o' the woods. It just ain't safe for a man to open his mouth around here. I keep gettin' my foot stuck in it."

"I'm not going to ask you to explain all that," she said, giggling as she slowed for a group of cyclists.

"How 'bout we start again, and I'll do my best to tone down my more colorful speech?" he proposed, twisting in his seatbelt to grin at her. "You asked if I lived in a big city. The answer is yes. Nashville's population is over a million people and its growin' as we speak. You ain't never heard of Nashville, right?"

She shook her head.

Eddie looked surprised. "Wow. Well, I reckon there aren't many country music fans here in France. Not that I'm a huge lover of that particular music genre either, it's just unusual to meet someone who's never heard of the Grand Ole Opry…" He stopped and squinted at her. "You haven't, right? Heard of it?"

"No. I 'ave no idea what you're talking about."

"That's kind of refreshin'," he mused. "Anyway, I grew up there. My daddy moved to Nashville when he was only seventeen. Thought he'd make it big as a country/western singer and become a star. Instead, he ended up sellin' used cars, singin' in run down honky-tonks on the weekends, and drinkin' too much. My mama had a rough life with him." The smile faded from Eddie's face. Perhaps that was the reason why he wasn't fond of the music. Elyse sought to turn the conversation to happier topics.

"I am sorry to 'ear that," she said. "Do you 'ave sisters or brothers? You said you don't see much of your daughter."

"Naw. I was an only child. Both my parents are gone now, but I ain't complainin'. Life just ain't fair sometimes. The important thing is to remember that when we're given lemons we have to turn around and use 'em to make lemonade. Right?"

"*Oui*," Elyse said. She wasn't exactly sure what he meant about lemons, but was in complete agreement about life sometimes being unfair. "So, your company is based there? In Nashville?"

"It is," he said proudly. "It's one of the biggest importers of olive oil in the United States. And the U.S. is the largest importer of olive oil in the world. We bring in about 375,000 metric tons each year. Not my company alone, mind you," he amended, "but throughout the country as a whole." He pointed to a grove of pale green, silvery trees as they passed.

"I had no idea what olive trees even looked like before I came here last fall and spent time with your son. He's a good man. Raphaël too."

"*Oui*," Elyse agreed, watching an oncoming car and navigating through one of the many roundabouts on the backroads of France.

"You have a daughter too, right?" he asked.

"Lia," Elyse supplied. "She is a teacher and lives in Marseille with 'er 'usband and my two grandchildren, Maxine and Marcel. We see them often."

"I look forward to meetin' 'em." He cast her a sidelong look and pushed his glasses up his nose. "If it works out that way, I mean. No tellin' how long it'll take to get a new passport and credit cards. Might happen real quick-like."

Elyse signalled, turned, and smoothly accelerated along a quieter road, lined with family-run vineyards. She found herself hoping it would take a long while for Eddie's personal items to be restored, and then shook herself. What was she thinking? No matter how attractive he was, she wasn't interested in starting a relationship with a man, least of all this stranger.

"True," she said. "But my experience 'as been that such things take time. We will 'ope it does not, of course. You must be anxious to continue your business trip. However, if you are 'ere in a weeks' time, this Saturday, there will be a party at the chateau to welcome the new baby. You are most welcome to join us."

"Thanks," he said with feeling. "Y'all have been so kind and generous to help out and let me stay with you. I can't tell you how much it means."

"*Vous êtes les bienvenus*. You are welcome," she said, flashing him a grin. "You might as well learn a little French while you are 'ere."

"*Bienvenue*." He said the word as though he were tasting *fois gras* for the first time; rolling it around on his tongue, savouring the flavours. Only then he delivered the morsel with an almost perfect accent and grinned at her. "I'd like that."

They were well into the Luberon now. It was rich countryside, resplendent with creamy-white hilltop villages, lavender fields, olive groves, and daily markets, all bathed in the brilliant sunshine of Provence. Rolling hills, thickly carpeted with oak, pine, cypress, and the sweet scented garrigue, stretched into the distance as far as the eye could see. Orchards, their fruit long since picked and their leaves preparing to turn shades of rich ruddy reds and oranges, flashed by the car windows as they sped along.

"It's real pretty here," Eddie murmured. "I figure it wouldn't be hard to live in a place like this."

"*Oui*." Elyse agreed. "Each area and village holds a charm all its own. Many sightseers come for an 'oliday and find themselves searching for an 'ome to purchase and put down roots. I think Provence 'as that effect on people." She glanced at Eddie's profile as he gazed at the passing scenery. He had an aristocratic nose, she decided; not too large, straight with a small deviation at the tip from an old scar. It perfectly suited his strong jawline and high forehead. She liked the laugh lines at the corners of his eyes too. They spoke to a life well-lived.

Aware she was spending too much time considering Eddie's appearance rather than concentrating on the road, she gave herself a mental shake. Honestly! What was happening to her?

The long stone wall of an ancient property loomed high beside them sprouting lichen and other hardy plants. Behind it, buildings made of the same cream-coloured stone sat sturdily against the rustic landscape, their roofs covered in classic curved, red terracotta.

Ahead, she saw the first few signs of the town. They had arrived. Elyse glanced in her rear-view mirror and waited as a motorcycle zoomed precariously between her and an oncoming motorist. The bike was going at least twice the prescribed speed, before entering the roundabout just outside the village.

"Whoa!" Eddie said, clutching the armrest and lurching forward to watch as the motorcyclist leaned into the bend almost perpendicular to the road, extending one knee to steady the bike on the pavement before shooting out the other side. "That was some crazy driving! Do they often do that around here?"

Elyse shrugged. "*Malheureusement oui*. Unfortunately, yes." She followed her French with the English interpretation. "There are many deaths due to such antics, but it does not deter them. So, one must be cautious if there are motorcyclists on the road." Taking the first right, she manoeuvred down a one-way lane with tall, adjoined homes lining the way. Ivy spread its lush tentacles across many of the buildings and hung low over doorways. Powder blue shutters were closed against the heat.

Driving further along, businesses began to appear. Colourful awnings announced the names of restaurants and long wooden signs, tacked to corners or over doorways pointed buyers to art studios, *boulangeries*, clothing boutiques, and giftware.

They continued on, finally coming to a point where the lane branched into two and a small square filled with people. Broad sidewalks were on every corner, filled with tables and chairs where people were eating. More of them spilled into the street licking ice cream, walking arm-in-arm, or just meandering from shop to shop on this lovely day. She slowed the car to a crawl as they inched their way through the throngs of holidaymakers and angled to the left.

The lane narrowed even more. It was made almost impossible to traverse due to racks of postcards, pottery, knick-knacks, souvenirs, decorative plants, and easels of artwork. Eddie sat up straighter, his head swivelling back and forth as he took it all in.

"What an interesting place," he breathed.

"This is Lourmarin," she said. As they edged beneath an arch, Elyse even wondered if the sides of the car would rub the walls. After escaping without incident, they entered one of the main avenues of the village. Deftly, she pulled forward and backed into a parking spot, amazed there was one free. She applied the brakes, turned off the engine, and sat back with a huff of air. Elyse didn't want to admit it, but her nerves were a little frazzled from driving through so many tight spaces. Taking a deep breath, she unfastened her seatbelt and leaned forward to point.

"Look over there." Obligingly, Eddie craned his neck to peer in the direction she indicated.

"Looks like a castle," he said, turning to search her face for clarification.

"*Oui*. It is Château de Lourmarin, built in the 15th century." She grabbed her floppy hat and scrunched it onto her head, then reached for the door handle and climbed out. Leaving the air-conditioned car and stepping into the warmth of an August afternoon was like walking into a wall of heat. She could see Eddie lift a hand to wipe across his brow almost immediately.

She met him on the sidewalk behind the car. "You should 'ave an 'at to wear, "she said with concern as she tugged at her brim. "Why don't we walk into the village and get you one. There is a shop quite close by."

Eddie shook his head and frowned. "No. I don't want you spending money on me, Elyse. I'll be fine. Nashville ain't close to the Arctic, you know. I'm used to hot temperatures. Don't you worry none 'bout me." Eddie lifted a hand to shade his eyes and looked around. "Where are we headed?"

"*Très bien*. As you wish" She lifted a shoulder in resignation. "I thought, per'aps you would like to stroll through the chateau, and I will tell you a little of the 'istory of this area. It is quite fascinating."

For his answer, Eddie in a flourish bowed low and swept

an arm to indicate that she should precede him. "After you milady," he said with old-world gallantry.

"*Merci Monsieur.*" She giggled, almost feeling like a schoolgirl again with his attention. He fell into step with her as Elyse led them up the hill to the imposing edifice.

"So, that's a chateau, hey?" said Eddie, scratching his chin. "But you call your house a chateau too, right? Yet this place looks older and bigger than your home. It's more like what people think of as a castle. What's the difference?"

"*Eh, oui*, I should try to explain. Our chateau is an 'ome, a place of residence that 'as passed from generation to generation for several 'undred years. Therefore it 'as the designation of chateau. This…" she said, pausing to spread her arms wide to encompass the structure on the hill before them, "was built on the ruins of a fortress dating from the 12th century and it's the first renaissance castle in Provence. It's a true chateau, or castle as you say, typical of the medieval period, and 'as fortifications to withstand attack."

Eddie smiled down at her and crooked his arm, holding it out for her to take. "I can see you're the right gal to have along as my tour guide," he said, running the other hand through his hair to keep it off his face. "So, your chateau… estate…whatever it's called, is it all yours? Or does it belong to your sons? It's a pretty big operation."

Elyse considered it for a moment. Acquaintances, almost strangers really, didn't usually ask such personal questions and it was rather startling. She supposed it was the American way. And he was such a forthright man.

She looked at his proffered arm and slid her hand tentatively inside. This intimacy made their excursion feel special, like a date. She was hesitant, but told herself they were simply two acquaintances out for some sightseeing. It meant nothing.

"I suppose Chateau de Belliveau belongs to me in the legal sense of the word," she answered after a time. "My 'usband, Georges, took it over when 'is father died, and when 'e passed away, it became mine to carry on as a legacy for the next generation. Yet, as you know, my sons run it without much input from me."

"And they do a damned fine job too!" Eddie said with emphasis.

Rounding a bend, they came to a gravel walkway beneath the intermittent shade of cypress trees and crunched their way to the arched stone entry.

Eddie began to protest when he saw Elyse reach for her purse to pay their admission. Despite that, she waved his objections away, then handed him a ticket and plasticized brochure that explained each room they would be seeing.

"Don't be silly," she said when they passed through the gate and found themselves alone. "You 'ave no way to pay at the moment, through no fault of your own. I want you to see this chateau. Let us think no more of money from now on. One day, when you 'ave everything sorted out, you may do the same for someone else in need. Pay it forward. Is that not what you say in America?" She winked at him. "*D'accord?*"

"If *d'accord* means, do I agree, then yes, I agree. I'll do as you say from now on. I can't thank you enough for all you're helping me with." Once again, Eddie spoke the French word with a perfect accent.

They walked beside a small, rectangular pool bordered with flower beds and almost completely covered in lily pads. A fine mist blew from a cooling system nearby and as if on cue, they stopped beneath it. He caught her hand in his much larger one and turned her to face him.

"Your kindness will never be forgotten, and will most

certainly be repaid," he said, his voice deepening. Catching her eyes with his own, he lifted her hand and gently pressed his lips to her skin. Elyse felt her breath catch in her throat as the touch of his mouth sent shivers up her spine. Releasing her, he stepped back. Yet the cornflower blue of his eyes held her captive until he blinked, breaking the spell, and she turned away in confusion.

"I—I think the self-guided tour begins around the corner," she said, hurrying away. Raising a hand, she felt each of her cheeks and knew they must be flaming red. She forced her heart to return to a normal pace and began to tell him what she knew of the place.

"A man from one of the oldest noble families in Provence built this chateau, but after the French Revolution, the estate passed from owner to owner. The owners were primarily interested in the land rather than the building. And so, it fell into ruin until 1920 when an industrialist from Lyon bought it at auction and took a long while to restore the chateau to its former beauty."

By this time, she had taken Eddie through to a circular area with rooms leading in several directions and a staircase winding up. Climbing the stairs, they entered the first chamber and consulted the large, laminated cards they'd been given to determine where they were. The rooms were filled with period furnishings and art. Elyse had been to the chateau before, but appreciated it just as much the second time through. She looked at Eddie from beneath her lashes. Was he enjoying their outing?

Slowly, they made their way throughout Château de Lourmarin. They only paused to examine the artifacts and discussed how their cards revealed that the castle was still used for exhibitions and concerts.

"I wonder if there are any events coming up in the near

future?" Eddie pondered, holding his chin and tapping a thoughtful finger on his upper lip. "It would be a nice thing for us to do." He looked at her with a hopeful smile and then suddenly groaned. His shoulders slumped. "What am I saying?" he muttered. "I can't ask you out on a date without money to pay your way…Damn it!"

Elyse's heart went out to him. "Please, do not worry yourself," she said, laying a soothing hand on his arm. "What 'appened was beyond your control. *Pas de problème*." She smiled with what she hoped was reassurance. "If there are no concerts 'ere, there will be events elsewhere in the Luberon that we may attend. I would like that very much."

It was only as they were leaving that Elyse realized what he had said. A date. Had she agreed to go on, what he had called, 'a date?' How did that happen? She needed to explain to him that they were friends, nothing more. It felt as though she were getting caught up in a whirlwind beyond her control and it scared her a little. Although not as much as she had thought it would. Part of her, deep down inside was thrilled with the attention.

However, she found herself getting close to this man, and far too quickly. An image of Armand slipped unbidden into her mind. What would he think of this? *I turned him down one day and am 'dating' another man the next.* Sadness washed over her. She hoped he would never have to know.

They wandered back into the sunshine and exited through a different door, closer to where she'd parked the car.

Eddie squinted at his watch and then at the sky. "That sun is unrelenting," he said shortly. "Does it ever rain?"

Elyse laughed. "*Bien sûr*. Of course, it rains. Although not as much as other parts of the country. November is the wettest month, I believe. 'Ow many times 'ave you been to France? 'Ave you seen other parts of the country?"

"Last year was my first trip…anywhere outside of the United States, and I came here to Provence." Eddie held out his arm again and Elyse threaded her own through it without reservation. "Needless to say, when the boss asked if someone wanted to go again, I was first to raise my hand."

A group of teenagers straggled toward them, laughing and pushing one another. Eddie steered her to one side, shielding her until the young people had passed. His thigh brushed hers, and as they resumed their course. She felt herself blushing, yet again.

Feeling she must hide this sudden awareness of his proximity, she began to speak quickly. "I imagine it would be quite an opportunity to take a trip that your company pays for and visit parts of the world you wouldn't get to see otherwise. I haven't been to the United States myself, but I've been to Canada. Quebec to be exact. And before I was married, I travelled throughout Europe with friends. Would you like some ice cream?" she blurted at the end, worried she was rambling.

His eyebrows shot up. "Ice cream? Well, sure that would be real nice. Thank you kindly." As they passed the car and continued strolling through the little town, Eddie came closer, leaning in to whisper into her ear. Elyse could feel the tickle of his breath in her hair and the closeness of his body. Again, her heartbeat quickened. *C'est ridicule!* She forced herself to act naturally and focus on his words.

"I'm just wonderin' if this place we're goin' to might have facilities. My eyeballs are floatin'."

"Tu blagues!" she protested in loud French before she considered the English equivalent. Stopping dead, she took a hurried step backwards. "I mean, you must be joking.

What are you saying? That your eyes are floating? Do you need a doctor? Are those the facilities you speak of?"

Eddie smiled and waved to a couple that strolled past. They cast curious looks at him and Elyse. "Nothin' to see here, folks," he told them, and then frowned as they shot him a bewildered look, gave him a wide berth, and hurried away. "Guess they don't understand me anyway."

He put a hand to his mouth to stifle a laugh and then guffawed loudly. "I just can't seem to watch what I say. In Tennessee, there's a lot of colourful sayings and I grew up with 'em all. That was my dad for you. He had a sayin' for every occasion. This one just means," he leaned close and whispered again, "I need to find a toilet." He lifted his index finger to eyebrow level and ran it back and forth. "Get it? Too much coffee this mornin'. I'm plumb full up to the eyeballs."

Elyse got it this time. Her mouth opened in a silent 'O,' and she grinned. "Per'aps you should 'ave a second job creating a dictionary, so people like me can decipher what you are saying." Crooking her finger at him she said, "Follow me."

She quickened her pace, and they strode along the contracted street, dodging families, children, cyclists, and cars until they came to her favourite little café. She'd been here alone several times and spied a tiny table for two. It was outside, but set back from the busy street.

"The toilet is inside on the right and down a corkscrew staircase," she said. "I will order something for us to start with. Per'aps not a drink." She winked at him. "What flavour of ice cream do you like?"

"Nothing too exciting," he said over his shoulder, grinning as he turned to go inside. "Chocolate will do."

A young man paused at the table with a loaded tray of

dirty dishes balanced on one hand to take their order. She asked for her two favourite flavours and the chocolate for Eddie. The server nodded and hurried away looking hot and tired in his black pants, long-sleeved white shirt, and apron tied tightly around his middle.

Elyse sat back and rested her head on the wall behind her. She took off her hat to use as a fan and pushed a few strands of hair from her forehead. Adjusting her sunglasses, she looked at the milling throng on the street and thought how very comfortable she felt with Eddie. He was easy to be with. Absently, she considered what the two of them might do with the rest of their afternoon, before they headed home to join the family for the first meal prepared by Madame Laurent.

She rolled her eyes just thinking of the formidable woman and found herself wondering what Madame Laurent's little granddaughter would be like. A small child running amok in the kitchen or tearing through the garden on a bicycle was not an appealing thought. She caught herself. Armand must have faith in her, and good reason to send his aunt to fill in for him. The woman couldn't be as bad as appearances had led Elyse to believe this morning.

She shifted her thoughts to the remainder of the day. From having done a couple of them by herself before, she knew of several nice walks in the *forêt de cèdres* between Lourmarin and Bonnieux, a picturesque village to the northwest. It would be perfect, she decided, almost rubbing her hands together with anticipation. They could go for a quiet walk in the shade of the forest.

Sobering, she recalled walking there with only one other person…Armand. It was his idea that they went, since it was one of his favourite places to escape the hustle and bustle of life. The shady path was hard to find, but that only added to its charm. It wound along the base of the mountain and followed a trickling stream, which made it a peaceful place to wander among the cedars and connect with nature.

At the end of the walk, they'd come to an abandoned estate. Armand had told her why the lovely old mansion, pool, and surrounding grounds sat alone and forsaken, slowly succumbing to decay.

On that day they had talked for hours; each of them revealing their innermost secrets and dreams. She had confided her sorrow at losing Georges, her greatest fears, and the hopes she clung to for her children and her life, never thinking for a moment that Armand might be developing feelings for her. He had been her closest friend, she realized, but she had never considered him as anything more. And now he was gone. It left an ache in her chest.

With an effort she considered the trail through the cedar forest, *sans* Armand. It would be a perfect place to go today.

The waiter appeared at her left elbow, jolting her from her reverie. He set two glass bowls, frosty from the cold, creamy scoops of ice cream within, on the table along with spoons and napkins. At the same moment, Eddie walked through the restaurant door on her right.

"*Merci*," she said to the young man as he moved to clean the next table.

"Just in time, I see," Eddie said, slipping into the chair next to her. "It looks fabulous. Thank you so much Elyse. When all of my credit cards are sorted out, I'll pay you back every penny."

Elyse picked up a napkin and spread it across her lap before wagging a reproving finger at him. "We agreed, remember? No more discussion of money." She slid her small silver spoon into the pistachio half of her treat and then added a little of the coffee flavoured portion to the same mouthful.

"Mmm," she rolled her eyes with enjoyment as it melted on her tongue. "You must try another flavour next time, along with your chocolate. I know of one other place to take you where the owner makes the ice cream 'erself. It is *délicieuse. N'est-ce pas?*"

"*Oui, d'accord.*"

To her surprise, Eddie had answered correctly. A very good guess, she surmised.

"I'm a fast learner," he said, and licked his lips. "This really is excellent. But if you're gonna try to teach me some French, it seems only right I share a few sayings from the Deep South with y'all."

Elyse nodded, her mouth too full to reply. She dabbed at her lips with the cloth napkin and waited for his first lesson. Although he'd used so many outlandish phrases already that it might be best if he explained a few of those instead of adding more.

He sat back in his chair, regarding her with a smile as he lowered his spoon and swallowed. "I think you're pretty as a peach and the cat's meow all rolled into one," he said.

"Are you teaching me colourful sayings or trying to flatter me into ordering another round of ice cream?" she asked with a laugh. "I understand what a reference to the beauty of a ripe peach would be, but the meowing cat 'as me baffled." Using her spoon, she scraped up the remaining cream and popped it into her mouth. His sweet talk made her a little uncomfortable, so she tried to turn it into a joke.

"They both mean the same thing," he explained. "Something, or in this case, someone, is very appealing to me."

71

Elyse blushed as she met the intensity of his gaze. He leaned his elbows on the table and came closer.

"Why are you still single, Elyse? You're not only beautiful, but you're also smart, intelligent, have a kind and loving heart, and a great sense of humour. Why has no one come around to snap you up?"

She sniffed at his familiarity. This man did not hesitate to ask such personal questions. "If by snapping me up, you mean why 'as no man claimed me like some sort of prize specimen to place on 'is shelf…simple, it is because I wish to be free. I 'ave not been interested in any man since the passing of my 'usband, Georges."

"Guess that came out wrong," Eddie leaned back and hastened to correct himself. He laid a hand over hers on the table. "Sorry if I offended you, Elyse. Please forgive me. I only said it because I find myself drawn to you and it made me wonder if there was anyone else in your life…" His voice trailed off.

She pulled her hand away, then busied herself with laying her napkin on the table and motioning for the bill. The discussion was getting a little too personal, and the warmth of his hand had sent a tingle of awareness up her arm. This man was quickly getting too close again. It was time for them to do something completely different.

"I 'ave a hike planned for us," she said, clearing her throat.

Following her lead, he dropped the subject. "In this blazing heat?"

"No. Well, actually, yes, but it won't be so 'ot where I am taking you." She glanced at her watch, realizing it was 2:30 and all they'd had for lunch was ice cream. "I thought we could stop at a wonderful *boulangerie* I know and pick up sandwiches and drinks. Then, I know of a lovely walk beneath the cedars where it is shady and cool. There is an abandoned house along the path which makes it interesting. We can eat our lunch and be back 'ome in a few hours for the evening meal." She ventured a look at him, having noticed that he'd sat back and folded his arms across his chest.

"Why sure. I reckon that sounds like a great idea." He scooped up the last of his melting ice cream and beamed at her. "Ain't nothin' like havin' dessert first."

Chapter Six

Elyse and Eddie motored out of town in the opposite direction from which they'd come. Eddie held a paper bag containing *un sandwich au jambon*, sliced deftly in half by the server for them to share. Also, inside were lemon tarts topped with raspberries in a cardboard box, and two bottles of cold water.

It was the perfect lunch. Elyse knew how foreigners raved over the crunchy, French baguettes with their soft, fluffy interiors. When you coupled that with a thin layer of fresh butter and a few slices of ham, it was perfection. Her mouth watered just thinking about it. And the tarts had been irresistible to her, despite already having eaten ice cream.

She threw him a sideways glance, then kept her eyes on the road. "It's not far," she said, "but the road is rather narrow and curvy from now on, so I must take care. During the summer it gets busy with visitors."

Eddie nodded. Leaning forward, he looked at the mountains rising around them; craggy outcrops of creamy-white stone visible among the trees. "Way back I used to take my daughter for hikes," he said suddenly. "We'd go campin' at the Bledsoe Creek National Park every summer. It's only about forty-five minutes from Nashville and pretty as a picture. Angie, that's my daughter, she loved fishin' in Old Hickory Lake."

Elyse listened. He sounded sad, as though the weight of the world rested on his shoulders and for the second time, she wondered why he hadn't seen his girl in several years. Did she dare ask?

"It sounds like you were close with Angie when she was young," she said after a few moments.

"Yep. We were close. Especially after her mother died. She was only ten years old at the time. It was hard, but we did okay." He sighed, unfolding and re-folding the paper bag on his lap. "It was about three years later when everything fell apart. Sometimes life takes a turn you don't expect," he finished cryptically.

She felt his eyes on her and, though she was heading toward a hairpin curve, she chanced a look at the man. His face looked anguished, she thought with a jolt. Except he turned quickly away, wrestling with the bag again and hiding his face.

"What 'appened?" she asked, before she could stop herself. It really wasn't her business, and she bit her lip angrily, but he didn't seem to mind the question although his response was evasive.

"I was..." he paused as though searching for the right words, "taken away on business unexpectedly...for a few years. Angie never forgave me. I missed her weddin'," he said, sorrow causing his voice to roughen. "It would've been nice to walk her down the aisle. But…" he sat up straighter and took a deep breath. "What's done is done. We had some good years. Who knows, maybe one day she'll forgive her old man." He forced cheerfulness into his voice and changed the subject.

"Do you like fishin'?"

The question raised an image in Elyse's mind that made her inwardly giggle. Her? Fishing? She pictured herself in long rubber boots, a plaid shirt, a bucket hat lined with hooks, and dungarees standing thigh-deep in a river with hopes of landing a googly-eyed trout. She wasn't quite sure what dungarees even were, but thought she'd read somewhere that people in North America wore them while fishing.

Was that her? No. It would never be her. Yet it was clear that Eddie must enjoy this particular pastime and she didn't want to sound disparaging.

"No. I 'ave eaten the fish, but I 'ave never done the catching," she smiled, but kept her eyes fixed on the road. They were almost at the tiny pullout where she would park, and she needed to stay vigilant because it wasn't easy to spot. Plus, the road was increasingly curved, and she had a motorcycle following at an unhealthy distance.

"I'll have to take you sometime," Eddie said, as though he was promising her a visit to Buckingham Palace. "You'd love it."

They rounded a tight curve and the road widened into a space only big enough for two cars to park. Elyse signalled and then braked carefully, keeping an eye on the traffic behind. The car crunched over large, white stones and came to a halt.

"*Voilà*," she said, turning off the engine. "We 'ave

arrived." She breathed a sigh of relief that she had success-fully navigated the winding road and opened her door, stretching as she stood. It wasn't a long journey, but she had been tense behind the wheel.

She pointed to the nearly invisible trail entrance. Eddie, carrying their lunch, followed her into the trees. It was as lovely as she remembered. The scent of pine was heady, and the trail was littered with the accumulation of dried needles from countless years, muffling their footsteps. Only small patches of dappled sunlight filtered through the canopy above, enveloping them in a tranquil atmosphere. Although there wasn't any breeze, the temperature had dropped by several degrees.

"This is real nice," Eddie said from behind.

"I am 'appy you like it. The spot I 'ave in mind for our picnic is just ahead."

They came to a clearing where a little arched stone bridge spanned what must be a torrent of water at certain times of the year, but currently was only a gurgling stream you could jump across. Bees hummed happily in patches of sunlight and one lone sunbeam caught the bridge where ivy had not claimed the ancient rock. Elyse hurried to it and bent to brush leaves and debris away.

"I thought we could sit 'ere," she said. Straightening, she peered at Eddie's face. Would he appreciate the seclusion and rustic beauty of their impromptu dining area, or was he someone who required a proper table and chairs to eat?

"It's great," he enthused. Moving to her, he caught her hand and squeezed gently. "Thanks for bringing me here," he said. "I can tell it's a special place to you. And you shared it with me, that means a lot."

She was pleased. They settled down on the bridge, their

legs dangling, and bit into the crusty sandwiches, breathing in fresh air and listening to the sound of silence. Elyse stole a look at her companion as he chewed with contentment. Maybe life could be good again.

After they washed the last of the flakey pastry down with the now tepid water, they got to their feet and brushed the crumbs from their clothes. Eddie crumpled the bag and stuffed it into his back pocket.

"Shall we continue," he asked, and bowed gallantly to indicate she should lead the way.

Grinning, she stepped off along the path, ferns and small shrubs parting as she pushed through the lush fronds. Near the stream, the forest floor was cool and damp, despite the oppressive heat above the canopy. Though thanks to the cedars and sturdy oak, they were spared.

"What do you do in your spare time?" Eddie asked. "I know you work on the estate, but what do you enjoy doin'?"

Elyse didn't hesitate. "I like to work in my garden," she said over her shoulder. The path broadened and she stopped, to wait for him, so they could walk side by side. "I love to sift earth through my fingers and feel the joy of watching seeds grow and thrive." She tucked her hair behind an ear, so she could see him better. "And you?"

"What? Besides fishin'?" he joked. When she smiled, he continued. "I like dancin'. Learned that from my mother. She used to say a man that can't lead his partner in a waltz ain't good for much." He grinned across at Elyse. "Oh, and I like tinkerin' with cars, I suppose."

"Tinker-in?" Elyse was lost again.

"Fixin' em. Especially old cars," he supplied. "Them new ones have too many gadgets and computer chips for a guy like me."

"Were you close with your mother?" Elyse asked. She

couldn't ask knowledgeable questions about car repairs or fishing techniques, but a woman that insisted her son learn to waltz, and taught him herself, was intriguing.

His face took on a faraway look and he stared along the path as though seeing a time long ago. "Yep," he said shortly. "She was a gem. Selfless, you know? Always doin' stuff for other people and my useless father in particular. She never gave a thought for herself." He shoved his hands into the pockets of his trousers. "And look where that got her."

"Where?"

"Dead. That's where," he answered roughly. He stopped and physically shook himself. "Sorry. I don't know why I'm tellin' you this. It's water under the bridge. Just makes me sad thinkin' about it. Cause it wouldn't have happened if it weren't for him. Guess I feel comfortable sharin' with you, but I didn't mean to sound so angry. My mother was a wonderful woman and I loved her dearly. She died too young is all." He tried to muster a smile, but his lips curled into more of a grimace. "Tell me about your family."

"I grew up in the Luberon, the area of France we are in." Elyse caught the tops of some tall grass in her hand and let them swish through her fingertips as she walked. "My father worked as a *professeur d'histoire au lycée*, a history teacher. I believe it is why my daughter Lia was drawn to the occupation. He spent much of 'is time poring over books in 'is study and was devoted to 'is students, but 'e was a good 'usband and father. *Ma mère* stayed 'ome with my brother and me. She loved us and I loved 'er. We 'ad a wholesome life." She shrugged. "I was 'appy."

"A world apart," Eddie murmured.

"Pardon?"

"Sorry." Eddie flashed her a grin, all traces of the bitterness that had darkened his face was gone. "I was thinking out loud. We grew up around the same time, but lead vastly different lives. I'm glad yours was better than mine. Do you have a favourite childhood memory?"

Elyse thought about it. Images swam before her eyes of her younger brother and herself. Despite their five year difference in age, they had been close and remained so into adulthood. "Sundays in summer," she said emphatically. "It didn't matter what was 'appening in the world, or whether my father 'ad work that needed doing…Sundays were for family. Aliens could 'ave landed in the garden or zombies taken over the world, my father would still 'ave gotten out the car, my mother would 'ave packed a lunch and we would 'ave gone somewhere to 'ear live music. Or we would 'ave driven to the Mediterranean to swim or laid on rocks warmed by the sun near the Pont du Gard to watch stars twinkling over the two-thousand-year-old Roman aqueduct."

"Well butter mah butt and call me a biscuit!" Eddie announced loudly. "Y'all have the best memories I ever did hear." He waved a hand around his ear to shoo away a wasp.

Elyse laughed outright at this. For the first time, she didn't need any explanation for one of his sayings. It was hilarious though and it took a few seconds before she could ask him the same question. She felt a little trepidation in doing so, since his past appeared to bring up a host of unpleasant memories. But it seemed only polite to inquire, because he had asked her.

"Yes, I got me one," he said quickly. "I was about eight and climbed into an old pickup of mah dad's that was sittin' in the driveway. It's important to note that the driveway was on a real steep slope." He grinned at her, holding back a low-hanging branch for Elyse to pass. "Unfortunately, he'd left the keys in the ignition. Naturally I started the engine and managed to release the brake 'cause I'd watched him do it about a million times. I was so busy tryin' to reach the clutch that I didn't notice the truck was rollin' backwards at a pretty fast clip. By the time I looked out the window, it was out onto the street and pickin' up speed." He paused to chuckle.

"I'd never seen my father move so fast," he continued. "He galloped up to the door of that truck, ripped it open, and leaped inside like he was an Olympic hurdler. Once he got the vehicle stopped, he grabbed me and shook me till mah teeth rattled." Eddie's voice trailed away, and Elyse glanced at him. His face was shadowed and drawn. This was what he considered a *good* memory?

He took a deep breath. "I thought I was gonna be thrashed. Wouldn't have been the first time he beat me, or my mother, but…he didn't. He pulled me close and held me for a long time, right there in the middle of the street. That's the one and only time my father ever hugged me. So yeah," he turned and gave her a watery smile, "that's a good memory."

Elyse smiled back, but inwardly she felt sadness wash over her. To have known so little love from his father must have been awful. Perhaps it was part of the reason for the break between his daughter and himself. Maybe Eddie didn't know how to be a father.

Without warning, they broke out of the trees and onto a track, overgrown with weeds. Elyse recalled the spot and led the way down until she spotted the deserted mansion, hunkering behind a tangle of trees.

"Through here," she said. Bending, Elyse forced her way through a thick hedge and burst into what used to be

81

the back garden of the estate. A long, concrete pool lay to her left with a wide lounge area all the way round. Straight ahead was a small, ramshackle building. She and Armand hadn't explored any further than the exterior of the house when they'd been here before, and she was curious to look around.

Eddie gave a low whistle. "Wow. You said it had been deserted, but this is somethin' else! Why would anyone leave a place this grand to just rot away?" He walked to the edge of the pool and stood beside her, staring down into years of leaves, dirt, and debris. A mangled deck chair was curled up in one corner, with the bleached blue, nylon strips of seating torn and scattered about the space.

"French laws," Elyse answered shortly. "It belonged to an actress who 'ad achieved fame in France and around the world back in the 1950s," Elyse explained. "When she got older, she built this chateau deep in the woods of the Luberon as a retreat from the world. After 'er death it was divided between her two children, but they could not agree. One wanted to sell, the other wanted to keep the home. There was arguing and court battles until neither of them would speak to each other. And so, nothing could be done with it. As a consequence…" she swung her arm wide to encompass the estate before she continued, "the property fell into ruin. Now no one can enjoy it."

"What a shame," he said. They left the pool to walk across to the little shack. Deep fissures ran across one side of the lounge area where Hollywood's elite would once have gathered, splitting open a chasm where weeds had sprung through. A few bottles still cluttered a wooden bar where there had been a barbeque, sink, and shelves filled with rows of glasses and other dishes, most of them broken on the ground. Rickety stools laid broken at their feet, but one still stood erect, and Elyse slid onto it. She brushed away dead leaves and rested her head in her hands with her elbows on the counter.

Eddie rounded the bar. "What'll ya have, madame?" he said, picking up a cracked glass and polishing it on his sleeve in an attempt at humour. "Whiskey? Pastis? One of our fine wines, perhaps?"

Elyse chuckled. "I trust you implicitly, good sir," she said, batting her eyes. "You may decide for me, as I'm far too busy studying the lines for my new movie."

Eddie's face fell as though she'd said something wrong. "You trust me?" he asked. "Elyse you're joking, right?"

An uncomfortable silence enveloped them. "Of course," she said lightly. "You're the barman, aren't you?" But he hadn't been joking when he'd asked her that strange question, and she turned away feeling puzzled.

"Come," she said, turning away in hopes of breaking the tension. "Let's go look at the 'ouse." They walked alongside the pool until they came to a tall picket fence that ran around the perimeter of the dwelling. Vines and young oak entwined it creating an impenetrable barrier. Elyse pushed back through the hedge and onto the old road.

She fought off an eerie feeling. It was as though the ghost of the long dead actress still roamed the premises. A shiver travelled the length of her spine and back up again. She stole a look at Eddie who had come to stand with her at the gate leading to the front door. His face was impassive, but it was clear that he was shaken by the oppressive shadows that hung about the building too.

It was an impressive three stories high, with six windows like empty eyes staring blankly into space along each level. A broad veranda ran the full length of the bottom floor. Two large, latticed windows, still with lacy curtains hanging limply across, looked upon an overgrown world. The white paint was peeling and dirty, and the classic blue shutters that covered every window were broken and faded. A few dangled from rusted hardware. It was dilapidated and sad, but there was something more. Elyse hadn't felt it the last time she was here.

"It's amazin' that the windows haven't been broken," Eddie murmured, almost to himself. He leaned on the fence, wrapping both hands around the peeling posts of the gate, a half-smile on his face. "Kids back home would have destroyed this place."

"I suppose not many people know about it. It isn't close to a village." Elyse wrapped her arms around her body. She felt cold, regardless of the temperature.

"Shall we go?" she asked, trying not to sound anxious.

"Sure." Eddie turned away immediately. Elyse sensed that he had been affected too, but perhaps in a different way. She didn't want to contemplate it and realized that no matter how comfortable she'd felt with him this day, Eddie was still a stranger.

With hasty steps, Elyse walked to the path and plunged along it, her head down, wanting to rid herself of this feeling she didn't understand. They marched like this for some time until he called to her.

"Hey, what's your hurry?" Panting a little, he jogged up beside her where the path had once again widened. "Oh, I get it. You probably can't wait to get back home and spend some time with your new cook?"

She laughed, coming to a stop and resting her hands on her hips as she waited for him to join her. "You noticed?"

"Pretty hard not to," he admitted. "That woman's scowl could stop traffic, and she gave you quite a few. Any idea why?"

"I might have one." Elyse said. The heaviness had lifted, and she continued walking beside Eddie at a slower pace.

"Well, if you can figure out her problem that'd be good. Until then, I'd try to be around when she's dishin' up yer plate 'cause I think it might be poisoned."

Elyse laughed again. "Surely, it's not that bad. But you're right. There's no rush to get back." Fishing a phone from inside the crossbody bag that was always with her, she checked the time. "Four o'clock. Hmmm…On Tuesdays in the summer, there's an evening market in Lourmarin. I think you might enjoy it. I can pick up some fresh produce to appease Madame Laurent and everyone is 'appy. *D'accord?*"

"*D'accord*," he said, offering his arm.

She took it willingly and felt a thrill of the closeness she had noticed earlier. However, she wasn't about to delve into her thoughts about Marie Laurent with him. After all, the woman was Armand's aunt and as such, she deserved respect, at least for now.

Elyse parked the car in a large lot to her right as they entered Lourmarin once more. It was a bit of a walk to the *marché* from here, but parking spots were hard to come by in the summer. She was grateful to have found one. She wedged her little car into the tight spot, reached for her hat, her purse, and the shopping bag she always carried in the back seat. Together they clambered out.

The sun was lower in the sky now and lent a rosy glow to the massive plane trees that shaded the area. They crunched through the chalky gravel at the edge of the hard-packed clay lot and climbed a short flight of stairs to the main level. People passed them carrying shopping bags filled with vegetables peeking from the tops—the long feathery fronds of carrots, stalks of celery, and leafy ends of beets. Others clutched bottles of both olive oil and wine or buried their faces in steaming crêpes wrapped in paper. Children licked ice cream cones and dogs frolicked at the end of leads. It was a family scene filled with tourists and locals alike.

They followed an equal number of people who were making their way toward the scene as were leaving and this time Elyse didn't wait for Eddie to extend his elbow. She grasped his arm and linked her own with his. He looked down at her, his eyes crinkling at the corners as a warm smile lit his face. Patting the hand that she laid on his fore-arm, he rubbed an absent-minded thumb in lazy circles on her skin. It felt good, she decided even though it surprised her. Almost as if they had always walked this way.

The *Lourmarin marché* was packed with people. Elyse led the way up a final set of steps to a paved area marking the main square lined with trees. The businesses were all open and filled with customers. At the center, however, were the many individuals who set up canopies with handmade merchandise laden tables beneath. They displayed a vast array of cheeses, fresh vegetables, hand woven baskets, kitchenware made from olive wood, clothing, handbags, *saucisses fumées*, and an assortment of lovely pottery.

Slowly, she and Eddie took a turn around the square peering at every offering and exchanging a smile whenever something took their fancy. Buyers were tempted by nougat, the sweet, sticky slabs of creamy white sweetness studded with almonds and pistachios. Mounded bowls of succulent green, red, and black olives filled tables till they groaned under the weight. Some varieties were mixed with herbs, whole cloves of garlic, slivers of red pimento, or chunks of feta cheese, while others were marinated in hot, spicy oils and other sauces. At the next stall, barrels of fragrant lavender seeds hunched beside a farmer to be scooped into tiny mauve bags, while lavender soap, hand cream, and honey lined his table.

It was a feast for the eyes. Elyse always enjoyed market day and peeked at Eddie to catch his expression. The crush of people was too great for them to walk side by side and he snatched at her hand as she was sucked into a crowd of people waiting in a que to enter a popular restaurant. He tugged her free, laughing, and, still clutching her palm, he threaded his way through the throng. Eddie swung his head around to look at her. He couldn't contain his excitement. His eyes were wide, darting to and fro to take it all in.

"I had no idea it would be like this," he shouted over the mob. "What an experience."

"*Oui*," she called back. "It is not always quite this way, but in summer there are many visitors. Could you please angle us toward the farmer with the onions tied into clumps and hung over 'is stall."

He gestured in the direction of a white van with a red and blue awning pulled from its side and a table strewn with every sort of vegetable imaginable underneath. Elyse nodded. People stepped in front of him and around him as he pushed through the masses. Eddie was broad-shouldered and good-looking, causing several women to look at him twice. Elyse noted it and smiled to herself.

When they reached the stall, he dropped her hand and picked up a massive head of green cabbage, hefting its weight in his hands.

Elyse spoke to the heavily moustached vendor in French and asked for two bunches of carrots, a leek, three kilos of red potatoes, and the cabbage that Eddie still held. She thrust her shopping bag toward him. The man deftly weighed and bagged the items before charging her and handing them to Eddie with a smile.

"*Merci beaucoup monsieur*," she said.

"*Oui, merci beaucoup*." To her surprise, Eddie echoed her perfectly. He lifted the wicker bag and patted it with a smile.

"*De rien*," the seller said cheerily before greeting his next customer with the same jovial aplomb. Elyse eyed the vegetables. She loved the fact that she was directly supporting the farmers and artisans rather than lining the pockets of the middlemen.

"Shall we go?" she asked, bringing out her phone to check the time. One missed call. She flicked it on to see who it was and if they'd left a message. It wasn't surprising that she'd missed a call. Service was always sketchy in the forest, particularly when drawing near to the mountain, which was where the old mansion was located. She saw it was her friend, Louise, and it had been followed by a text to assure her the call wasn't urgent. Her eyes flicked to the hour and realized it was getting late. Dinner was usually served at 19:00 and it would take forty-five minutes to get home.

With the extra traffic both coming and going from the market, it took more time to leave Lourmarin. By now, Elyse was getting a little anxious. She always liked to be home to talk with her family over the evening meal, and particularly now with the new baby in the house. She didn't want to miss seeing Celeste. And what would Marie do about dinner? She should be at the chateau.

Seizing the steering wheel as though her life depended on it, her body tightened, and she stepped on the gas. The vehicle lurched into a roundabout causing an oncoming car to honk. Elyse jumped and swerved. Maybe she wasn't as confident a driver as she had thought. She shot out the other side feeling wobbly.

Eddie reached across the console of the car and laid a steadying hand on her arm.

"Hey, there's no rush," he said reassuringly. "This woman, Madam Laurent, could start an argument in an empty house. She'll make a meal with or without you and I'd hazard a guess that she'd rather it be without you anyhow." He leaned forward to look into her face. "My point is...don't worry about gettin' back there. You're the matriarch of that there establishment. Your family will wait till you arrive to start. No problem."

Elyse loosened her grip. "You're right," she said, looking at him in a mix of relief and astonishment. Why had she allowed herself to get so worked up? "*Merci.*"

They arrived at Chateau de Belliveau forty minutes later, the remainder of the trip having been spent in companionable discussion. Now that she was back, Elyse felt eager to see baby Celeste, but apprehensive when she thought of the formidable cook that Armand had set in place. She didn't want to have an altercation with Armand's aunt, but neither would she tolerate a hostile takeover in her own kitchen.

She grabbed her purse and after ensuring Eddie had the carrier bag of produce, she hurried down a path between rows of knee-high box hedge and around the back of the house. She couldn't wait a moment longer to see what Madame Marie was up to.

Glowing golden in the lowering sun, the surface of the pool glimmered like a mirror as she walked by. The water looked inviting after a long trudge. Maybe later she'd indulge. She crossed the patio and plunged into the herb garden, stooping to pull an errant weed. Some habits never die, she thought grimly, tossing the plant into a wheelbarrow as she passed.

"You're on a mission," Eddie remarked from behind her. But she didn't slow down until the sound of whistling broke into the evening air and the marvelous aroma of barbequed meat wafted to her twitching nostrils. She stopped short at the sight of Raphaël with a set of silver tongs, conducting an invisible orchestra over the closed lid of the outdoor grill. He turned as she came into view, yanking headphones from his ears with a slight look of embarrassment.

"*Salut ma mère*," he said, setting down the implement and stepping forward to kiss her cheeks. "*Et Monsieur* Wright, 'ow nice to see you." He made no attempt to greet Eddie with *la bise*, the traditional French greeting, but he nodded with a broad grin.

Elyse's heart warmed as she gazed upon her youngest son. His dark hair was getting long again and as was always the case, began to curl in the most endearing way. His dark brown eyes, set off by the turquoise blue of his t-shirt, danced with laughter.

"You caught me," he said, moving to pick up his tongs and wave them over his head. Catching Eddie's eye, he explained. "I played the clarinet in school and always thought I'd be in an orchestra."

"Nothin' wrong with that," said Eddie. "We all have dreams. I wanted to be a race car driver, but instead I'm a vegetable handler." He shifted the bag to his other arm and smiled.

Elyse giggled. "Eddie and I stopped at a market," she explained, pointing at the sack. "What are you cooking?" She moved to stand next to her son and he lifted the lid of the barbeque. Smoke billowed out and the meat sizzled.

"I'm not paying attention to my job," he said with a furtive glance toward the kitchen window. "Madame will 'ave my head." He began flipping steaks, causing flames to *whoosh* up and lick the meat.

"Good luck," said Eddie, as he followed Elyse inside.

Elyse opened the door with a flourish and darted in, half expecting to see the surly woman on her way outside to berate Raphaël for his inattentiveness. But instead, a scene of complete serenity greeted her.

Marie Laurent was humming to herself as she slashed the tops off steaming baked potatoes and scooped the fluffy insides into a bowl.

"'Allo," she said with a smile, turning to welcome them. "Your son, Raphaël, 'as been so kind as to 'elp me with the meal preparation. It will be a simple meal tonight, but I was assured that you like steak."

"*Oui c'est vrai.*" Elyse was so surprised, she forgot to use English. "I mean to say," she corrected, looking at Eddie and lifting her hands, palms up in a gesture of shock, "it's true. One of my favourite meals is steak and baked potatoes. Especially stuffed," she added.

"*Bien,*" the lady said, resuming her work. "It will be ready in thirty minutes."

Feeling a bit dazed, Elyse motioned that Eddie should place the things they'd bought on the counter.

"Madame Laurent, I…" Elyse began.

"My name is Marie, *s'il vous plait,*" the lady interrupted.

"Very well," Elyse continued. "Marie, I purchased a few fresh vegetables at a market this afternoon. I 'ope they can be useful to you."

"*Merci bien!*" Maria beamed at Elyse, but didn't leave her task. "I will look at them later. As I said, dinner will be served in 'alf an 'our."

Dismissed and bemused, Elyse beckoned to Eddie, and they went through to the dining room.

"Can you believe the change in that woman?" she whispered.

"Maybe she just had to settle in," he suggested.

Hearing deep laughter, they hurried to the salon where Julien was still chuckling. He sat next to Angelina on the sofa, cradling his tiny daughter. Chubby little legs protruded from one of the soft, white cotton rompers Elyse had bought for her. He stood to place the baby in her arms. Elyse was thrilled. Celeste kicked jerkily and cooed as Elyse cuddled her, whispering words of love.

The four of them chatted about the day's events. Julien had spent most of his day repairing the machinery needed to begin pressing olives later in the year. One vital piece of the equipment had failed to operate properly.

Angelina told them how she had given Celeste a bath.

"I think I ended up wetter than her," she finished with a laugh. "What a fiasco." She reached for one of Celeste's chubby little feet and gave it a kiss. "What did you two do today?" she asked, looking at Elyse.

"We went for a lovely walk around Lourmarin, visited the chateau, and the market. Then we hiked through part of the *Forêt de cèdres*. Armand took me there once..." Her voice trailed away as her mind touched on the painful subject of Armand's sudden departure.

"It was an interesting day," Eddie cut in, filling the awkward gap. "I hope we can do it again real soon."

"Why don't you take Eddie for more sightseeing tomorrow?" Julien suggested. "I think we 'ave quite a few days ahead in which to discuss our business."

"That would be great!" Eddie was enthusiastic, looking at Elyse. His blue eyes captured hers with such happy anticipation that she was pleased. He appeared to have enjoyed their day as much as she had.

Raphaël appeared in the doorway.

"If you don't mind a little charcoal," he said, looking hopeful. "Dinner is ready."

The meal was delicious. Corn on the cob and a garden salad with homemade vinaigrette also accompanied cheesy potatoes and slightly charred steaks. Then, just as everyone was pushing away from the table, replete, Maria stomped into the dining room bearing a tray filled with tiny glistening pots of crème brûlée. The crack of spoons breaking the sugary crust filled the air and there was laughter all round as Marie stood beaming at them from the doorway, arms crossed over her ample bosom.

"I'll tidy the kitchen first, and go to bed," she announced after everyone took their first creamy mouthful. "It's been a long day, but I'm 'appy to be 'ere. Armand was right. You are a good family."

Elyse was again taken aback. Was this really the same grumpy woman she had met this morning? Of course, the woman had only been ill-tempered with her. The true test would be when the two of them were alone.

"Oh la la," Marie said, returning a few seconds later. "I forgot to remind you that my granddaughter will be arriving in two days…with Armand. *Est-ce que ça va?* Can I 'ave the time off to meet 'er train with 'im?"

"*Bien sûr, pas de problème,*" Julien assured her. "Of course, the little girl must not be left alone any longer than necessary. Will she 'ave to be back to school soon? It is almost September, after all."

"*Non, non,*" Marie said, waving a dismissive hand. "*Elle est mannequin pour Dior de Paris. Elle a vingt ans.*" The new chef whisked out of sight leaving the table to digest her final remarks, looking at one another in amazement.

Eddie, who was seated beside Elyse, leaned over and whispered. "What did she say?"

"She said 'er granddaughter is not a child. She's a twenty-year-old model for Dior of Paris."

Chapter Seven

The next morning, Elyse came downstairs to find Eddie on the patio, basking in the early morning sunshine with a coffee in one hand and the local newspaper in the other.

"Good morning, *bonjour!*" he cried, scraping his chair back to rise to his feet. Folding the paper, he tucked it under his arm looking genuinely happy to see her. Elyse felt a pleasant warmth spread through her.

"*Bonjour*, Eddie," she said. With a flourish of gallantry, he pulled out the chair next to his, and bowed, but she didn't sit down just yet. There was a slight breeze this morning, and the chiffon ruffles of her tangerine top fluttered. She felt pretty today, and had taken extra care with her makeup, even adding a lipstick that matched the blouse. She'd belted a tan-coloured flowing knee-length skirt at her narrow waist and slipped on a pair of simple, strappy wedge sandals to complete her outfit.

"You look beautiful, Elyse," he said, still standing. His eyes traveled her full length before resting on her face with an appreciative smile.

Colour stole up her cheeks and she drew his attention back to what he'd been doing.

"Any shocking developments in the world," she said, pointing at the newspaper. "'Ow can you read it when the words are all in French?

"Naw. Just the usual problems," he laid it on the table. "And I mostly just look at the pictures as I wait for my gorgeous companion. Can I get you a coffee?"

"*Merci.*' Again, Elyse felt a little off-balance at his remark. She decided to ignore it. "But I will stop in the kitchen on the way as I always take a walk through my garden in the morning. Would you like to accompany me?"

For his answer, he pushed both chairs back and stood to attention. "You have only to say the word," he quipped, extending the crook of his arm as he had done the day before.

She slid her arm through his, feeling a thrill as she came in contact with the lean contours of his middle. Together they promenaded through the garden. Elyse breathed deeply, closing her eyes. The busy hum of the bees and the scents of rosemary and thyme, warmed in the morning sun, filtered through her brain, giving it peace.

"It's nice here," he said. Eddie ran his hand down the rough bark of a young oak as they walked farther away from the vegetable garden. "You've done a lot of work to create such a place."

"I didn't do it alone." An image of Armand working alongside her, popped into her mind and she gave herself a mental shake. "My 'usband 'ired a gardener to help us in the beginning and then our chef, Armand, spent time out 'ere every day, 'elping me."

"This man was more than just your chef, wasn't he?" Eddie's eyes scanned her face.

"Armand was—is my very good friend," she corrected herself and sighed before she could stop it.

"Not more than a friend?" he asked. "'Cause I don't want to be steppin' on anyone's toes."

She stopped and disentangled her arm from his in order to pull a few weeds that were encroaching upon the flowers they were passing.

"Stepping on toes...?" she sent him a quizzical look as she straightened.

Eddie waved an expansive arm through the air. "I mean, if you and this guy are a romantic couple, I don't want to interf—"

"No!" her reply was so quick that she cut him off. "We're friends. That's all." She'd answered with too much speed, she knew, but nothing could be done about it now.

Eddie frowned. "Well, if you're sure," he said. "'Cause you're the kind of lady that a man dreams of meeting... intelligent, witty, warm, loving, family-oriented, and real pretty, too. I'd be a fool not to want to spend as much time as possible with you."

A surge of heat warmed her face that had nothing to do with the sun. She didn't know what to say to this unexpected outburst. Yet, she didn't feel uncomfortable with it, as she had when Armand had said almost the same things. Her heart warmed to this man and as he smiled down at her she tucked her hand back into his waiting arm and squeezed him close. She didn't refer to what he'd said, but thanked him in general.

"*Merci beaucoup*. And what would you like to do today? I assume you 'ave not 'eard anything about your passport?"

"Naw. I gave 'em the phone number here and mine as well. My company is involved too, so something should happen soon. Until then, I'm all yours." Eddie covered her hand, where it rested on his forearm, with his other hand and pulled her close. Their hips bumped and a shiver went through Elyse like an electric shock.

"I like you a lot, Elyse" he said, continuing his unabashed honesty. "I'm hopin' we can be more than friends."

Suddenly the colours of her garden looked brighter and her heart flooded with emotion. Could this be her second chance at love?

"I think I'd like that too," she said softly.

Scenery whizzed past the Audi as Elyse steered toward the tiny village, they'd been so close to the day before, Bonnieux. After a hurried breakfast of croissants and coffee, alone, they hadn't wasted any time in leaving for the day's outing.

The Luberon Valley spread before them once more, the rolling hills of oak and cedar giving way to orchards, vineyards, and olive groves that radiated vitality in the light of the ever-present sun. At times the trees closed in on either side of the road. Even through the car's closed windows the loud chorus of the cicadas could be heard as the insects established their territory and called to females.

Yesterday, Elyse had enjoyed spending time with a man she was romantically attracted to, something she'd thought would never happen again. Since her husband's death, she had closed herself off from the idea of another chance at love. Yet, she and Eddie had chatted animatedly the whole time. He appeared as interested in learning about her as she was in knowing him. Words and laughter had come easily, which surprised her since she was a reserved person. She normally preferred to know someone well before sharing family anecdotes and observations on life.

She smiled inwardly, anticipating the day ahead with enthusiasm. Although the route she took them on was the same, through Lourmarin, she didn't drive straight to her destination. Instead, she took them down a winding road into the high country, to the tops of the mountainous landscape where lavender fields had recently flourished, and goats grazed.

At one point she drove the car down a grassy lane and stopped near the wide, welcoming branches of an ancient oak. On one side of them, a man guided a flock of goats across the road and into another pasture. His faithful dog kept a watchful eye on the herd's progress. The black and white Border collie barely shot the car a glance. With its tongue lolling, the animal trotted to and fro behind the bleating goats until, pushing and shoving one another, they bolted through a gate. Swiftly, the man shut it behind them.

On the other side, a late field of lavender had been cut into prickly, purple rows. An area of the thick stalks had been gathered into bundles and tied with a coarse brown twine, then piled in a fragrant violet-coloured heap. She rolled down her window to luxuriate in the scene, hoping Eddie would appreciate the beauty that surrounded them. The hot sun heated the dusky heads of the lavender, flooding the air with their intense perfume.

Elyse stepped out of the car and into the warm embrace of the French countryside. She breathed deep, feeling truly alive and connected to the country of her birth. Birds sang from the treetops beside them, and the distant clang of bells, dangling from the necks of the goats, provided the perfect ambience.

She looked at Eddie. He leaned against the passenger

door and crossed his arms, lifting his face to the sky. He took a long breath before looking across the roof of the car to catch her eye.

"It's gorgeous," he said in awe. "Like a postcard, or a picture in a calendar. Not something you expect to see while out for a casual drive." He turned to face her, leaning his arms on the roof. "Thanks for bringing me. I'd have never known it was here if not for y'all."

"*Du rien*. You are welcome," she shrugged. "I love it up 'ere. If we did not 'ave the family estate..." Elyse swayed her head back and forth, considering, "this would be where I would like to live." Reaching into the car, she grabbed her hat, slammed the door, and wandered under the shade of the enormous tree. Apart from the farmer with his goats, there wasn't a house or another soul in sight and she stretched out her hands to feel the rough bark of the tree feeling a rush of happiness overtake her. Life was good.

Eddie, shading his eyes, walked toward her, his step purposeful, his eyes open in alarm. Without warning a dog began to bark from somewhere behind her. Whirling, she saw the short haired and stocky animal. Its fur stood on end like spikes along its back, teeth bared, and ears laid flat against its large head. It wasn't the collie they'd seen, but a burley, muscular animal that looked ready to attack.

Fear clutched at Elyse's throat, and she froze. Ever since an Alsatian had bitten her when she was five, she'd been afraid of dogs, but she'd never been so threatened by one since. She knew it was protecting the farmer's property, but that didn't help the situation when its master was nowhere in sight. The beast took a few steps closer, its eyes riveted on her, a deep growl replacing the bark. It slunk lower, gathering itself to spring when Eddie, with unhurried movements, stepped in front of her and turned sideways.

"Do as I say," he rasped in a low voice. "Do *not* look it in the eyes or run. Stay calm, don't yell, or scream, or turn away. Slowly back up to the car and get inside."

Elyse gulped, knowing the dog must sense her fear. With fumbling footsteps, she began to shuffle backward, feeling behind her for the hood of the car with a trembling hand. Ahead of her, Eddie moved too, but not so quickly. He spoke soothing words.

"There now. We didn't mean to bother you, now did we?" he said in a flat monotone. "This is your land, is it? Sorry we barged in and upset the applecart. We'll get out of your way as soon as we can lil' doggie. You just stay right there, don't move a muscle, and we'll be on our way. No one's gonna hurt you."

The dog held its ground. It growled menacingly, but didn't move any closer, which Elyse was grateful for. It cocked its head to one side, clearly listening to Eddie's words, yet the low rumble from deep in its chest continued.

She took tiny steps back until, after what seemed like an hour, she felt the smooth surface of the car's hood beneath her outstretched fingers. Elyse swallowed. She was almost there. Sliding her hand down the fender of the Audi, she willed herself to remain calm. Her hand fumbled over the side-view mirror and finally grasped the door handle.

Eddie wasn't quite to the front of the vehicle yet. He edged his way along, continuing the steady monologue he'd started. With deliberate, slow movements, Elyse opened the car door, pulled it just wide enough for her to fit, and slipped inside. She heaved a shuddering sigh of relief but then looked on in horror as Eddie appeared to trip. He went down, his arms flailing, and the dog leaped.

Elyse screamed. It was involuntary. She couldn't stop herself, but clapped a hand over her mouth and shrank in her seat. Eddie shot into view, flung himself across the hood of the car, over the windscreen, and onto the roof. The dog slammed its body on the front of the vehicle, its paws scrabbling for a foothold on the paint. It barked furiously. Elyse heard Eddie moving, then he slithered down the side of the car, wrenched open the passenger door and threw himself inside. He slammed the door shut just as the dog hurled itself against it. Panting, he stared straight ahead for a few moments.

"Well, that was intense," he said, announcing the obvious. The dog, now relieved of its guard duty, lifted a nose to the window at Eddie's shoulder and moved off to inspect the tires. Order had been restored.

"Thank you," Elyse breathed, once her racing heart had subsided. She gripped the steering wheel with both hands, her knuckles white. She leaned forward and rested her forehead on them. "I was bitten once, as a child and I 'ave much fear ever since. That was impressive. You saved me from an attack."

Eddie, red-faced and breathing heavily, shook his head. "Didn't know I could still move that fast," he admitted ruefully. He turned and his brow knitted together with concern. "You, okay?"

"*Oui, merci*. I am shaken, but so grateful you were with me. I fear that dog would 'ave torn me apart if not for your bravery."

"He was just protectin' his land," Eddie reached out and patted her knee, downplaying his role as her defender. "Still, it's pretty scary. When I was a kid, I worked at an animal shelter. Stuff like that happened sometimes. You learn how to deal with it." He lifted a careless shoulder. "Just glad I could help."

Eddie leaned across the console of the car and held out

his arms. "Come here," he commanded, a smile creasing his face. "I think you could do with a hug."

Elyse felt like gelatin, all wobbly and shaking like a leaf. Somehow, she pushed away from the wheel and allowed him to wrap his arms around her comfortingly. She rested her head on his shoulder and told herself to settle down. He had saved her. There was nothing more to fear. She shut her eyes for a moment, but still saw the dog's snarling face in her mind and snapped them open again.

He held her for a long moment before beginning to stroke her hair. She moved closer with a little moan of pleasure. It was a sure way to relax her, and Elyse grew less tense with each passing minute. Soon, Eddie sat back, cupped her chin in his hands and looked into her eyes with tenderness.

She felt herself melt. Whether it was from the fright she'd just had, or the hypnotic way his eyes seemed to caress her face, Elyse didn't know. Though when his lips gently touched hers, a warmth coursed through her body. Again, she closed her eyes, but this time it was to revel in the way his mouth moved against hers and in the masculine scent that enveloped her. Her hands lifted of their own accord to wrap themselves around his neck and curl into the hair above his collar.

He pulled away almost immediately, leaving her to wish for more, but his hands held her shoulders, keeping them apart as he smiled. She felt vulnerable and a little bemused as he pushed her back in her seat and held her hands tight.

"I think the farmer's comin' to see what we're up to," he said. "You might want to start the engine and we should leave. Are you alright to drive?"

She nodded, not trusting herself to speak. Was she fit to drive? Maybe, maybe not. She pressed the clutch and turned the key in the ignition. Her legs certainly hadn't regained their strength. They shook. Using both hands she rubbed briskly up and down her thighs, willing them to strengthen. Then she put the car into reverse and checked her mirrors before backing onto the main road. Eddie was right. The farmer was striding toward them with a long staff in his hand. The two dogs trotted beside him.

She rolled down the window and waved, calling to the man in an unsteady voice. "We only stopped to see the lavender," she explained in French. With a curt nod, the man stopped abruptly and went back the way he'd come with his dogs.

Elyse shifted into third as they continued on their way. She needed a coffee or perhaps a glass of wine would help to calm her nerves. She glanced surreptitiously at Eddie, but he was staring out the window. His kiss had affected her, but he appeared unmoved. Or was he?

"I'm taking us to Bonnieux," she said, pushing hair away from her face, determined to put the incident out of her mind. "We can 'ave lunch there and walk around the village."

"Sounds great," he said as he snapped his seatbelt into place. "Tell me about it."

"I don't know all the 'istory," she explained, "but I believe it is one of the most beautiful, perched villages in the Luberon. Bonnieux was built on a plateau and the 'ouses, some of them from the 16th century, spill down the 'illside in a jumble of earth-toned colours that make it quite charming to stroll through. The streets are steep, but there are fountains, many fine restaurants, and shops that make it popular. Especially in summer," she finished.

The road curved down one mountain and then ascended the next as she picked up speed, taking care to mind the blind corners since her French countrymen some-times passed on these curves. She applied her attention to the road and within fifteen minutes they were slowing as the way narrowed to a single lane. Seeing a red light ahead, Elyse geared down and rolled to a stop.

"That's odd," Eddie said, straining against his belt to crane his neck to the left. "What is this street? One way? There's no one coming and there's no lights over there," he gestured.

"*Oui*. The light is around the next corner. There is not room for two vehicles to pass on this street, so they allow only one to pass at a time."

Two small cars appeared around the bend and motored by them. Then the light changed to green, and Elyse released the clutch. Parking was located on the other side of the village. They passed people lounging at café tables next to the street while tourists trudged up the narrow sidewalks in sandals and shorts, mopping their brows in the heat. Cheerful red flowers sprang out of huge earthenware pots beside the road, and deep shades of fuchsia, soft pink, and white azaleas sprouted from above street level.

Elyse pulled into the parking area below the medieval center, near *la église neuve*, or the new church. Eddie crawled out and stretched, standing with hands on hips.

"What's goin' on over there?" he asked.

Elyse retrieved her hat, sunglasses, and purse from the back seat and shut the door before following his gaze. Under trees in the far corner of an open space beyond the parking lot, was what looked like an open gravelled area where a group of men were gathered. Some sat on wooden benches under scrawny trees while others held shiny silver balls, about the size of a grapefruit. More of the balls were scattered on the ground a few meters away from the assembly.

"It is *pétanque.* You 'ave not 'eard of it?"

One of the men leaned forward and swung his arm back, taking careful aim. Eddie shook his head as the loud crack of a metal ball slamming into more metal balls reached their ears.

"We, French love this game," she said. "It is a little like lawn bowling, I think." She noted, watching the group of older men playing. A heated argument broke out and someone stepped forward with a measuring tape. Elyse chuckled. "A small ball called a *cochonnet*, is thrown and then all the players try to get their ball closest to the *cochonnet.* There are often disagreements as to which ball is closest, as you can see. Each person does 'is best to knock the others out of play." She slung her bag over her head and settled it at her side before crunching through the gravel to the stairs that led up to the town.

"Those guys have got some stamina," Eddie said admiringly, falling into step behind her. "Bein' outside in the hottest part of the day."

Elyse merely smiled and tipped the brim of her hat a little lower to shade herself. "I know of a little restaurant," she said, checking the time on her wristwatch. "It should just be opening now for lunch. Their food is excellent."

Eddie caught her hand as they reached the top and laced his fingers with hers. A now familiar thrill shot along her arm at his touch and her heart hummed. They crossed a main road into town and strolled up a steep incline from the church to the next level of the village.

People, most of them tourists, were everywhere. As they reached the top of the incline there were several restaurants teeming with customers. The aroma of fire-roasted pizza wafted out to greet them.

Eddie looked at her with raised eyebrows.

"Not this one," she said, sending him a quizzical look. "You are 'ungry?'"

"Reckon I am," he said thoughtfully, pushing his glasses higher up his nose. "Just came on me all sudden-like."

His southern drawl was charming. Elyse almost skipped down the street. Instead, she tugged at his hand, pulling him onto the sidewalk as a car purred down the precipitous hill toward them. They passed tiny clothing shops and a *boulangerie* where the smell of fresh bread hit them in a wave of deliciousness. Eddie breathed it in with an exaggerated moan of delight. The shop window was bursting with a tantalizing array of baked goods from long, slender baguettes, croissants, delicate iced cakes, to tiny lemon tarts speckled with plump, red raspberries.

They rounded a corner, passing several other restaurants busy with patrons. She wagged a finger when he looked hopeful and led him around a corner and up a narrow, cobblestone passage. It was draped on either side with lush ivy and dotted with pots of hydrangea, azaleas, and even a few small olive trees.

Eventually, they passed under a stone archway and Elyse jabbed a finger over her head, pointing to it. "We are passing *sous* or under part of the restaurant now." A giggle burst from her lips as she watched his eyes widen and look up. He even ducked as though he expected the cook and his ovens to break through and crash to the stones at his feet.

She heard the clatter of plates and the clink of wine glasses as they proceeded up the incline. To their left, a black iron railing began, and white canvas umbrellas spread their shade into the tiny alley. They turned sharply and edged along the road into an open area where tables and chairs filled with customers covered the space.

"I should 'ave made a reservation," Elyse muttered, stopping short at the wide entrance of Brasserie St André, and peering inside for a server.

"*Bonjour madame*," said a young woman, appearing from the kitchen with a loaded tray of desserts and a selection of cheeses. "*Une table pour deux*?" She blew a wisp of hair from her eyes and smiled.

"*Oui s'il vous plait*," Elyse said.

"*Suis-moi*." The girl moved off among the tables and Elyse motioned to Eddie that he should follow her. They were lucky. The girl seated them in the far corner where the outdoor space narrowed to only enough room for their table. A moment later, their *serveuse* reappeared with two hand printed menu cards which she thrust at them before hurrying away. Elyse prepared to translate.

"Is there anything you do not like? Or do you 'ave allergies?" When Eddie shook his head, she pushed back in her chair and crossed her legs. "*Bien*. I think we should each order a *formule du jour*," she said, pursing her lips as she eyed the card.

"Sounds fine with me, whatever a for-mule is." Eddie leaned an elbow on the table and looked around appreciatively. "Nice place," he said. "Very, uh…French." He grinned at her as she traded her sunglasses for the reading glasses she always carried in her purse and peered at him.

"I believe there is a very good reason for that," she said dryly. "*Voila, une formule*, is a set price menu which includes a choice of starter, main dish, and dessert. You may order all three, or a variation of two, whichever you prefer. Sometimes there is even a drink included. It is a good value," she said, looking down to trace her two choices with an index finger.

"The first *formule*, is pork ribs with honey confit, mashed potatoes with locally produced olive oil, ratatouille, and an apple tarte. The second is French roast veal, ratatouille, crudités, salad, and fries with fresh apricot panna cotta."

"I bet that would sound real pretty if you said it in French," he urged, his grin broadening.

Elyse played along. She took a deep breath and began to speak at top speed. *"Côtes de porc au miel confit, purée de pommes de terre à l'huile d'olive du pays, ratatouille et tarte aux pommes. Ou, rôti de veau français, ratatouille, crudités, salade, et frites avec panna cotta aux abricots frais."* She finished with a sharp intake of breath. *"D'accord?"*

"Hold your horses," he cried, holding his hands in front of his face as a shield. "I'm plumb tuckered out just listenin'. Gimme that first one with the pork and I'll be happy," he said, running fingers through hair that stuck to his face in the heat. He squinted into the sun. "Sure is nice to have some shade."

Elyse laughed and waved to their server. "We are making progress," she announced. "I think I understand why you 'ave advised me to hold my 'orses."

After relaying their order in French to the server, she continued. "You could get used to the hot summers of Provence if you were 'ere long enough."

"I'm glad I have a chance to experience it," Eddie said. He leaned closer, his blue eyes rested on her. "But the sun isn't the only thing around here that's hot." He pushed back in his chair and grinned. He knew exactly what he was doing to her, she thought with a jolt of awareness.

She blushed and straightened her napkin with restless fingers, trying to think of something to say that would break the tension she felt. In the end she decided just to ignore his leading remark. "It would take a little time to accustom yourself to our weather…and per'aps 'aving a pool and an 'at would 'elp." She glanced up, holding his eyes without any sign of the discomfiture his words had caused her. "I insist on buying them for you once we 'ave finished our meal. After all, you saved me from that animal this morning." She shivered despite the heat they were discussing.

"I accept," he said promptly, grinning from ear to ear. "Although where we're gonna put that pool is anyone's guess."

Placing her elbows on the table, she rested her chin on folded hands and joined into the game. "A portable pool is too much?" She raised her eyebrows. "'Ow about a squirt gun and some sunscreen?"

"Perfect." They exchanged smiles that put her back at ease. "And you're welcome. I'd help you anytime, mi'lady," he added. "It was good I just happened to know what to do. Coulda gone either way really. We were both lucky."

Elyse decided it was time to introduce a new subject. Curiosity rose within her. "This company you work for, 'ave you been with them long?" she asked in a rush, looking into his face.

"About ten years now," he said. He relaxed, pushing back his chair and scrubbing a lean hand along his jawline. "Funny you should mention that because I've been thinking of leaving them. Maybe followin' a different path that involves my heart instead of my pocketbook."

"You 'ave?" Elyse was surprised. Concern for what he would reveal about his 'heart' gripped her. He had appeared so dedicated to learning how their olive oil operation worked and to delivering the best deal for his employer. Although, last year, despite the time he'd spent with them, no deal had ever been worked out. She'd never really asked Julien for the details, but supposed it would happen this fall, before the harvest.

"Yeah. I have a dream." He spoke carelessly, looking off into space as though he'd forgotten she was there. "It would cost a good chunk of money but…it would be worth it."

"What is it?" Elyse plunged in, regardless of what his response might be. "And do you 'ave this money?" Immediately Elyse felt she'd crossed the line. It was a personal question and none of her business. Yet Eddie answered her without batting an eye.

"Most of it," he gazed across the square and then sat up straight. "Look!" he said, staring and gesturing wildly.

Elyse looked. A family walked single file along the narrow sidewalk across from them, the mother pushing a baby stroller with an English pug squatting inside, and the father holding a long, taut lead, at the end of which was a straining child. "Do you see that?" he spluttered with laughter.

She saw it and nodded. They both subsided in giggles as the couple disappeared into a doorway. The server arrived with two glasses of wine on a tray and set them on their table.

"Cheers," Eddie said, thrusting out his dewy glass. "Here's to family diversity."

"*Oui. Et aussi pour ta santé,*" Elyse agreed, still chuckling as they clinked the thin crystal. "I also drink to your 'ealth," she explained. "But back to your dream. I would like to 'ear about it if you are comfortable telling me." She took a sip and nodded, encouraging him to continue talking.

"I have a hundred thousand," he admitted, setting his drink down and dabbing at his mouth with the linen serviette. "But I need three more to really make it viable. But that's doable. I just have to liquidate some other assets I have back in the States." He sighed, his face taking on a resigned expression. Then he rested both elbows on the table and leaned in like a conspirator. He looked from side to side as though there might be spies lurking in the shrubs that edged the perimeter.

"I'm thinking of retiring and moving to France," he said in a stage whisper. "I've been lookin' online, and I found a piece of land with an olive grove and a nice house near Nimes. It's nowhere near as grand as yours, of course, but it is beautiful. I'm just not sure if I can afford it." His voice caught. "Still, I'm determined to try. After workin' all my life and not bein' a proper father to my girl, I thought it would be a place to just relax and have her come spend time with me. To reconnect…ya know? All I want in life is a second chance with my child." Eddie looked so hopeful and sincere that Elyse's heart melted.

She blinked away moisture that sprang to her eyes. "Oh Eddie. That sounds like a lovely idea. Are you really serious about it?"

"As serious as I can get," he replied with an airy wave of his hand. "Angie, that's my daughter, well, she's always wanted to see France. I figure this is as good a way as any to get her to come stay with me for a while." He rolled the base of his wine glass in circles on the tablecloth, then took a deep gulp of the ruby red liquid. "It would mean a lot to me. I can't tell you how much. I just have to raise more money…" Eddie's voice was barely audible as he finished his last sentence.

Elyse took a sip of her wine, her thoughts racing. From what she knew of this man he was a true gentleman, acknowledged his mistakes, cared for his daughter, and was deeply troubled that their relationship had been severed.

She sincerely hoped, for him and Angie's sake, that he was able to realize his dream.

"I believe you will do it," she said, reaching out to touch his arm.

At that moment, their meals arrived. The steaming dishes were each placed with a thump onto the table before them. Eddie shook his napkin and laid it across his lap. He straightened his glasses and sent her a grateful look. All traces of the dreams he'd shared, and the pain he'd revealed concerning his estranged daughter, had been hidden away.

"Thank you," he said, picking up his knife and fork. "This looks delectable. You're a real friend, Elyse. Maybe, if I move here, we could continue to see one another." He held her gaze, tilted his head to one side and lifted a shoulder in an unsure manner.

He was a good man, and she was happy to be with him. Unbidden, a fleeting image of Armand crossed her mind. She'd enjoyed his company too. But the feelings she'd had for him weren't the same at all and inwardly, she shook herself. Besides it was in the past. Looking at this handsome man, his eyes crinkled at the corners with good humor and his lips parted into a smile, Elyse knew she was meant to be here—with Eddie.

"*Bien sûr*, of course," she answered without hesitation.

Chapter Eight

Elyse pushed away her plate and looked at her companion. He'd finished only seconds before her, rolling his eyes in rapture as he savoured the flakey apple tart.

"What a treat," he said, dabbing at his mouth and then laying the napkin beside his clean plate. "Every morsel was a taste sensation."

"I am so 'appy you liked it." Elyse almost felt as though she'd prepared the meal herself and was delighted to see his pleasure. As their dishes were cleared away, she asked for the bill and then told Eddie what she'd planned to show him next.

"Where that family disappeared to, just there," she pointed to the wide open gap along the stone wall opposite them, "is the beginning of a long climb to the top of the 'ill. The view is breathtaking and afterward we can continue on to *la vieille église* at the very pinnacle of the village. It is worth every one of the eighty-six steps, you will see," she assured him.

He sat back and patted his flat stomach. "Working off a little of this lunch is a good idea."

"*Bien, allons-y,*" she said, retrieving her wide-brimmed hat from the back of her wicker chair. She jammed it on her head.

She paid, thankful Eddie didn't lament the fact she was paying for their meal again, and his remorse at having no bank cards to handle it himself. She had never been in such a position as he was now and couldn't imagine being stranded in a foreign country. She had no doubt he would reimburse her later, but she intended to refuse it. This was the most fun she'd had in a long time.

He waited for her to join him and then extended his hand with a gentle, loving look on his face. She slipped her own inside, her breath catching as he lifted it to his lips.

"You are one special lady," he said. His eyes darted down to rest on her mouth, and she knew he wanted to kiss her. Except with a restaurant filled with interested spectators, perhaps this wasn't the time. His gaze flicked back to the patio as loud laughter broke out.

"Lead the way," he said, lowering her hand and facing the low arch across the street. Hand in hand they passed underneath, Eddie ducking his blond head. The path stretched before them, flat, cobblestoned, and slippery. "I'd hate to come up here in the rain," he remarked, as one of his feet slipped.

"There are 'ouses beside us," Elyse answered, waving a hand at the sheer stone walls on either side. "And people drive up 'ere to park their cars." The branches of a small tree curved over the path ahead and a wrought-iron lamp hung, suspended from an ornate hook above them.

"They do?" Eddie sounded amazed. He gave a low whistle as, sure enough, they passed an open area to the left where two small cars were parked in a fenced courtyard next to a flight of steps. "Amazing," he said under his breath. "Our vehicles and roads are so big in comparison."

"*Oui*. I 'ave been to Canada, as I mentioned before. It seemed to me that everyone drove large trucks. We rarely see *les camions* 'ere." They continued walking up the steep grade, with shrubs and trees spilling into the lane. Still there were no steps, only the flat stones, worn smooth from years of feet and other traffic. Doors and balconies, overhung by creeper, shrubs, flowers, and ivy jutted into the lane. It was lovely. Elyse took it all in through the fresh eyes of her friend as he exclaimed at every new sight.

Soon they reached the top. Elyse led him along a dusty road to a viewpoint surrounded by a concrete wall topped with a low pole fence. The valley spread before them in all its brilliant splendour. Silently they took it in as she and Eddie leaned on the top pole. Below the corrugated roofs of houses and businesses fanned toward the agricultural fields beyond, boasting poker-straight rows of vines, olive and fruit trees, or vegetables, as was the case. Roads snaked their way throughout and far across the valley was another hilltop village, perched on the very top of the hill.

"We are looking across the Calavon Valley," she said, raising her voice a little to be louder than the cicadas. She pulled her hat down and glanced at Eddie, holding both hands up to shade his eyes. She should find a shop when they went back down to the village and get him a hat and sunglasses.

"And that?" he asked, pointing to the village poised on the hilltop across the valley.

"Lacoste," she said. That village held a special place in her heart. Only a month ago, she and Armand had eaten dinner there late one evening. She sighed, the memory bringing a pang of sadness.

It had been beautiful that night, as they had sat on the terrace of Café de France. Together they had watched the gathering shadows of that magical hour between sunset and the rising of the moon over the Vaucluse Mountains. She could recall every bite she took, every shared moment, every word that passed between them as they waited for the moon to appear as a luminescent silver disc over the hilltop and cast its shimmering glow on the world below. The canopy overhead had been heavy with vines and strung with twinkling lights that winked at her from the greenery. And the chatter of satisfied guests had been merely a humming backdrop to the velvety night as it crept from the shadows.

But it wouldn't do to lapse into memories. She stood to attention, forcing herself back to the present. "It is Lacoste," she repeated. "We will go there next and 'ave a drink at a lovely restaurant I know of."

Eddie ran a hand across his glistening forehead. "What's the tall tower on that white hilltop over there?" he asked, looking out over the jagged tower of the lower church.

Elyse turned to look. "Ah yes," she said knowingly. "That is Mont Ventoux. I believe it is so named because of the French word for windy, *venteux*. Apparently, when the mistral blows, it can reach a speed of 320 kilometers per hour at the peak. The area was made famous after its inclusion into the Tour de France. You know of the cycling race?"

"Sure. Everyone's heard of it. So, they cycle up that monster?" Eddie whistled again. "You French have stamina, I'll say that much."

Elyse shrugged. "Anyway, the white you can see is limestone and the chapel is visible from 'ere. It was first built in the 15th century."

"You're better than a tour guide," Eddie said admiringly, looking down at her and slipping an arm around her shoulders.

She snorted, enjoying the feel of his embrace, but thinking about the reasons for her knowledge of the area. "I came 'ere often in the months after my 'usband died." She grimaced with a familiar stab of pain. "It was part of my 'ealing." She stepped away from him and said brightly, "Shall we continue to the top?"

Eddie said nothing, only nodding his acknowledgement of her explanation. He pushed a lock of errant hair from his forehead and bowed. "*Après vous madame.*"

He followed Elyse to the magnificent stone steps flanked by trees and shrubs that led to a crumbling arch covered in vines at the top. The steps were uneven and worn from the passage of many feet which, in Elyse's eyes, made it all the more lovely.

"I might sound like I am quoting from a website, but I wish for you to know that the original part of this old church dates back to the 10th century and was added onto during the 12th in a combination of Gothic and Romanesque styles. I love it 'ere and came last year at Christmas to view the Nativity scene which is quite outstanding."

Reaching the summit, they turned to the left and entered the church, pausing as their eyes adjusted to the shadowy interior.

A sense of reverence flooded Elyse's heart—such history. The spirits of parishioners who had worshiped here for hundreds of years filled this place. It was simple, yet its simplicity made it genuine. This church was a place where people had come to worship rather than to be awed by grandeur. Vaulted ceilings rose high above them, and plain, polished-wood pews stretched all the way to the altar. She moved further inside, walking along the aisle and looking back to take in the huge organ that filled the upper story over the door.

They said nothing. She appreciated Eddie's respect. After a few moments, in which they separated and wandered about the room, they met at the door and meandered back outside.

She crunched along the gravelly path surrounding the exterior of the edifice and came to a clearing made rough and gnarly by the ancient roots of the aged cedars that spread long sweeping branches overtop of two benches. They were alone. She strode toward the closest of the seats, sinking down to breathe in the scent of pine. Her ears rang with the sound of the cicadas and their scratchy, ever-present noise. She patted the spot next to her and Eddie seated himself so close, their bodies were in contact from knee to shoulder. It was not just the natural heat of the day that caused a flame to light in her chest.

She closed her eyes. A rush of emotion engulfed her, and Elyse wondered if she dared act on impulse. So, without another thought, she did. Turning, she took his face in her hands and pressed a kiss on his startled lips. Yet, he was so inflexible that her heart sank, and she tried to move back. But he caught her shoulders and pulled her close, his lips grazing her forehead, cheeks, and the tip of her nose with feathery caresses. Then he claimed her lips in a sweet passionate kiss. She melted against him, returning his kiss with an ardour that made her blush with remembrance later that night.

After long moments, he pulled away, to push tendrils of

hair from her face with a loving touch. He smiled, his eyes alight with desire, but he held himself in check, and realizing that caused her to draw closer. He was so considerate.

Eddie slipped an arm around her and tugged her even closer, if that were possible. She laid her arm along his leg. They sat like teenage lovers, staring out between the knobby arms of the trees, her head resting on his shoulder. She was at peace. If they could have stayed like this for the rest of time she would not have complained, but after a period of reflective silence, he stirred.

"Should we go, dearest? You said you wanted to take me to the neighbourin' village, correct?"

She straightened. He had called her, dearest. Her heart trilled. How wonderful. She sighed, her languor making it hard to care about the passage of such mundane things as minutes and hours. Time had slipped away on the wings of love.

With a jolt she realized what she was thinking. Love? No. It couldn't happen that quickly. Or could it? She thought of her son and Angelina. Even though they had taken several more months to get to know one another, they had identified their love within a week. And they were destined to be together for all time. However much they'd fought their feelings in the beginning, they had fallen in love almost immediately. Perhaps it was possible.

"Yes," she said with reluctance. "We should go, although it is so special here."

Eddie stood, his arm sliding from her shoulders to once again take her hand and help her to rise. Then he tugged her into his arms, one hand on the small of her back and the other around her ribcage. He held her so close she wasn't sure where she ended, and he began. Her body quivered with the sensations his body aroused in her.

"You are beautiful," he whispered into her hair, his breath tickling her ear. "I think I'm falling for you."

She echoed that sentiment, but didn't have a chance to tell him. Footsteps rattled on the gravel behind them, and he pulled away with a noticeable unwillingness. Instead, Elyse linked her arm with his, curling herself close to his body as they turned as one and began to retrace their steps down to the village.

When they burst out onto the street, she tugged at his arm, grinning. "Come this way. I want to get something for you."

"Get me something," he repeated. "No. You've done enough already." He resisted and they swung to a stop in the middle of the street.

"Unless you wish to be flattened by a passing motorist," she said with a glance up the road behind him, "I suggest you do as I say."

"Whoa. That almost sounded like a threat," Eddie laughed and allowed himself to be directed to a tiny shop she knew of just around the curve from the restaurant where they'd had lunch.

"Oh, it is." Elyse laughed in agreement. At this very moment, she didn't have a care in the world. She *really* liked this man. Perhaps it didn't make sense—but maybe love wasn't entirely sensible, and she wasn't about to let these moments slip through her hands. Life was too short, after all. Wasn't that what people always said?

She led him through the door of the tiny boutique by the hand and told him to stand by a full-length mirror while she selected two hats for him to try. He made a slight sound of protest, but did as she requested and turned to look at himself. She stood on tiptoes to place the first one on his head. It was a wide-brimmed, straw sun hat. He tipped it to the back of his head and made a comical face at his reflection.

"If I was on the label of a certain brand of coffee beans, wearin' a blanket over one shoulder and standin' beside a donkey—it would be perfect," he said consideringly. "A moustache would also help to complete the image," he grinned. "No, I don't think this one's me." He took it off and placed it on a shelf.

She giggled at his description. "*D'accord*. Try this." She handed him another. Again, it had a broad brim, but was made of a floppy cotton material with venting holes over each ear and a drawstring hanging beneath the chin. It flopped over his head, and he grimaced at Elyse in the mirror.

"What are you tryin' to do to me woman?" he barked, making a *faux* angry face. He ripped it from his head and gave a great belly laugh. "I look like a gosh-durn fool."

He was right, although she hated to admit it. The hat had given him a goofy appearance. No. It wouldn't do at all. Her fingers drummed a quick tattoo on her chin, and she narrowed her eyes to scan the room.

A saleslady stepped from behind a curtain and addressed them.

"*Désolé j'étais occupé.*" The woman apologized for her late appearance. "Can I 'elp you," she asked in stilted English with long pauses between each word. She appeared to assess the situation, then reached behind the cash desk, and lifted a tan-coloured, tightly woven, straw fedora from the wall. She handed it to Eddie with an air of confidence. "*Essayez celui-ci.*"

It had a thick brown leather band running round the middle and a rakish tilt to the brim.

"She says to try this one," Elyse interpreted, even though the clerk's meaning was perfectly obvious.

Eddie fitted it on his head and tipped it to one side. He spread his legs wide and placed his hands on his hips in a Superman pose. The style suited him perfectly. "I'll take it," he declared, whirling around to grab Elyse for a hug. "*Merci, ma chérie!*"

She gasped, unused to public displays of affection. Even Georges had never done such a thing. But she liked it, even when the saleswoman gave her a scandalized look.

"Do you carry clip-on sunglasses too?" she inquired, ignoring the woman's disapproval and smoothing the front of her pleated skirt.

The lady led them stiffly to the corner where a rack of the requested items was stacked. Eddie stepped forward to peruse the small selection. Clip-ons weren't that popular. As he twisted the rack and made his choices, she wondered how he had learned to say 'my darling' in perfect French.

He crouched down to use the tiny mirror, provided on the rack, and snapped a few pairs on. Finally, he decided on a style in a thin gold metal that covered his own quite handily. He looked like a whole new man. Pleasure welled up inside her as he struck another pose and chuckled. She'd always enjoyed shopping for others more than for herself.

Without further comment, the lady snipped off the price tags, Elyse paid, and they exited the shop. Eddie stopped on the sidewalk and looked up, pulling the brim of his new hat low.

"I dare you to do your worst," Eddie proclaimed, shaking his fist at the sun. "You have no power over me now."

He opened his arms to her. Laughing, Elyse flew into

them, and they embraced, right there in the center of town for all the world to see. Did she care? No. She might just fall in love with this man and his crazy, wonderful sense of humour.

Chapter Nine

Eddie rested a proprietary hand on her knee as the red Audi spun out of Bonnieux and headed toward their final destination of the day, Lacoste. She looked down at his large hand with wonder. Could this really be happening to her? Whether or not it could or should be happening—it was. And, for some reason it felt right.

She glanced at her watch. The hour was a little later than she'd hoped, since it would take time to see all the fabulous sights in the tiny town. She decided they didn't need to return home for dinner. Instead, she would text Angelina and ask her to inform Marie. Then, she and Eddie would eat at Café de France. The evening was the best time to be in Lacoste anyway, in her estimation.

They rounded the final curve before Lacoste sprang from the valley floor. The view from this direction always took her breath away. The buildings rose up the hill before them, their pale cream-coloured bricks glowing in the late afternoon sun. Amongst the green of the thick trees that shielded the hillside, each dwelling stood out starkly.

Elyse hoped she could find somewhere to leave the car. Lacoste, like the other stunning hill towns of the Luberon, was very popular at this time of year, and parking spots were at a premium. Yet, as they motored up the rise where the town began, she located an open spot.

"I thought we would eat 'ere this evening," she said as they walked up the hill she remembered so well. "Is that alright?"

"As long as I'm with you, I'm happy as a clam," Eddie declared, grabbing her hand.

Elyse found herself wondering whether clams were really all that thrilled with their lives, but decided it was yet another of Eddie's colourful sayings and let it be. First, she wanted to stop briefly at the café and make a reservation for seven o'clock, when it opened for the evening meal service. Then she wanted to take Eddie on the winding walk up the slanting, cobblestone paths to the top of the town where the ruins of a medieval fortress remained. She had stories to tell him about that too. Perhaps more than any other spot, because she loved it so well.

She left him standing out front while she took the few steps down to the reception area of the café and booked a table. Then she popped back up to street level. A thrill washed over her as she looked at the tall, strong figure waiting for her. He was a good-looking man. She noticed a woman sitting on the terrace of the Café de France openly staring at him as he stood there—for her. Her heart swelled with pride as she reached for Eddie's arm.

She guided him to walk along the edge of the main street as there were no sidewalks here. However, they quickly left it and began the long, winding ascent along the uneven cobblestones that wound throughout the village.

"*Donc*, I wi—" she began, but Eddie interrupted.

"Donk?" he repeated. "I know there's a lot of things I say that don't make sense to you, but…donk? What's that?"

Elyse found herself snickering as she did so often with this man. "Sorry. It is an unnecessary word, really. It means 'so.' But you interrupted me," she protested, giving his arm a little shake. "I was going to tell you some 'istory of what we are about to see."

"Sorry," he grinned, not looking sorry at all.

What a tease he was.

"Soo…" she began again, dragging the word out for emphasis. "Lacoste once lay in ruins due to the ravages of war and years of neglect. But as you can see," she waved an arm about her, "much 'as been done to restore its former charm."

"I do indeed see what you mean," Eddie agreed as they turned a corner at the top.

Elyse wanted Eddie to feel the antiquity of this place. It was easy to imagine yourself back in the Middle Ages when walking through the twisted corridors with the high stone walls dripping vines, since very little had changed over time. It was like strolling through a history book.

They climbed past a squat little house with brown shutters thrown wide and bright red geraniums teetering on shelves at the windows. Two ladies, their faces weathered from time spent beneath a relentless sun, followed one another out the door of this dwelling, and linked arms as they prepared to negotiate the steep lane. Each one wore nondescript clothes that were far too warm for the weather, heavy brown shoes, and had slung black purses over their arms.

Elyse hid a smile as she wished them a sedate, *"Bonsoir."* She paused to enjoy the purple and mauve colours of a hydrangea blooming profusely from an earthenware pot placed beside the door of the next house along their path. Lifting her phone, she took a picture and then launched back into her story.

"At the very top of the 'ill a castle was erected in the 11th century. Then in the 17th or 18th century it passed into the 'ands of the Marquis de Sade. More recently it belonged to a name that even you should recognise."

"*Even* me, hey," Eddie teased, giving her hand a squeeze.

She refused to give in to his bantering and continued with her story. "When the Marquis de Sade moved into the castle, 'e built a theatre able to accommodate 120 people so that 'e could perform the plays 'e wrote." Elyse lowered her voice to a loud whisper. "This man wrote many perverse, pornographic stories. At that time, 'is actions were scandalous and 'e was imprisoned for 'is writing, for brutalizing women, and for other reasons I don't know much about. 'Owever, I do believe the term, sadism, was derived from 'is name."

"Wow," exclaimed Eddie. "That's interesting."

They rounded a bend, meeting a group of noisy young people who jostled one another, four abreast, down the tiny cobblestone way.

Elyse stepped into an entryway and waited until they passed, watching Eddie's reaction to the boisterous crowd. Inwardly she wished she'd pulled him into the doorway with her. A flash of anger crossed his face as the teens bumped past him. He roughly elbowed his way between two young men, whirling around to scowl at the adolescents. They stopped short, several paces down from him and turned to shout obscenities in French.

"Watch where you're going, you bunch of useless punks!" Eddie hurled at them. His muscles stiffened, and his fists curled at his sides, ready to do battle. "Come back here and say that to my face. Maybe you need a lesson in respect."

Elyse froze in horror. Yes, the young people had been thoughtless and unobservant, but there was no reason to retaliate with such ferocity. They were just kids. She should do something, at the very least, perhaps step in and defuse the situation. But how? She was rooted to the spot.

Fortunately, the friends at the front of the pack hadn't noticed the kerfuffle. Their voices echoed off buildings as they continued to walk, laughing uproariously. This must have enticed the two boys to whirl about and hurry back to them, rather than fighting with Eddie on the hillside.

The confrontation had shocked Elyse. She tried to make sense of it, her heart racing as she sagged with relief. He just wasn't used to the aggressive crowds of summer, she told herself. Not like she was either. But she knew to be wary of people, young or old who were so intent on the sights, they neglected to watch where they were going.

Concerned with the scene she'd witnessed; Elyse grasped the corner of the entrance she'd been standing in and pulled herself out to continue up the path. Her legs were wobbly. She said nothing, still coming to terms with what she'd just witnessed.

Moments later, Eddie caught up to her. His features had returned to normal, with a smile on his face as though nothing had happened.

His demeanor felt equally bizarre.

"Please, continue with what you were saying," he said cheerfully, sounding eager to hear her tale. He made no move to take her hand though.

Following his lead, Elyse made no mention of the scene. Such incidents must be commonplace for him. Or perhaps this was how people from huge cities in the USA dealt with controversy. All she knew for certain was that she was unnerved. She felt unsure of everything she'd thought about this man.

She placed a hand over her heart, willing it to be calm for a few seconds longer before she picked up her story. "Most recently, Pierre Cardin, the name you will know," she said with a sidelong glance at Eddie, "purchased the Château. At the time of 'is death, it was bequeathed to the Institute de France which is comprised of writers, artists, and scientists. Cultural festivals, art shows, theatre productions, and concerts 'eld 'ere each year." Elyse babbled, speaking quickly. "Also, a renowned college of art and design moved in. They restored more of Lacoste too, and it acquired a prestigious reputation in the world of art."

"Thank you for sharing all that, Elyse," he said in a subdued tone. "It brings life to an area when you know more about the place." Eddie sighed and stopped. "But I need to account for my actions back there…and apologize to you."

They had reached a crumbling wall near the top of the town and a grassy area littered with large stones provided a spot for them to sit. She motioned that they do so.

"First, my forceful response was completely uncalled for," he said, seating himself on a piece of the wall. She remained standing as he held his head in both hands and stared at the ground. "I don't know what came over me. I'm truly sorry…" He looked up at her, his expression pleading. "I swear, I don't do that sort of thing. Ever. I don't pick fights with people, least of all kids." He shook his head with disbelief. "If we run into them again, I'll apologize to those boys too. In the meantime…can *you* forgive me?" he beseeched. Eddie reached out for her hand. When she gave it to him, he clasped it in both of his.

"*Je comprends*. I understand 'ow emotions can get away from us sometimes," she said. "Of course, I forgive you. Your instincts were on 'igh alert after the near dog attack this morning and you reacted without thinking clearly." Now that she recalled the dog attack it became quite reasonable.

A second wave of relief flooded her soul at his words. Okay, she had his explanation. While his actions were not ideal, he had acknowledged his mistake and would try to make amends. She couldn't fault a man for that. Elyse smiled and leaned back to pull him to his feet.

Eddie, his face lighting up, leapt to his feet and hugged her tight. "Thank you," he murmured into her hair.

"Let us walk to the top and then back down another way," she said, pulling away after a few moments, but retaining his hand. The world was right side up once more.

"By then it will be time for dinner," she noted with a glad heart.

Just before seven they wandered to the entrance of Café de France and were seated on the open-air terrace at a table for two. Elyse had requested this specific table since it afforded a fine outlook, but now wondered if it had been wise. It was the exact spot where she and Armand had sat together, and wonderful memories of that special night rushed back.

She determined not to let those thoughts intrude and turned her attention to the panoramic view. Just over the grey brick wall beside them, much of the valley was already in shadow. The mountain behind them, with the ruined castle at its peak, were etched against the farmland below as the fiery sun sank at their backs. In the distance, Bonnieux was bathed in a mantle of gold, the tall spire of the old church rising like a beacon above houses that spilled down the hillside in a jumble of stone. Beyond that was yet another mountain, huge and blue in the last light of day.

Elyse closed her eyes. The last of her tension ebbed away and was replaced by the perfect peace of the scene. She glanced at Eddie. He too was drinking it in. One elbow rested on the short wall beside him. He leaned over it and gazed into the orchards below, before his attention was also caught by the hill town opposite them.

"It's so pretty," he breathed. "Idyllic."

She agreed. Their server, a middle-aged man dressed in black with an apron tied around his waist, gave them a slight bow as he handed them the hand-written menu on a small chalkboard. It was short, and likely changed every day. But Elyse knew that was because everything they prepared was based on seasonality and freshness of ingredients. The chef was excellent. Even Armand had said so.

She propped the board at the edge of the table so Eddie could see it as well, even though she knew he couldn't read any of the words.

After skimming through the dishes that were offered this evening, she began the translation. She and Eddie both decided on the fresh gnocchi with parmesan, a light green salad, and peach panna cotta for dessert. She settled back in her chair and looked over the balcony.

In that short time the valley and the surrounding Vaucluse Mountains had plunged into a state of semi-darkness that left the world in soft shadows. But Elyse knew what would happen next and she was anticipating it with eagerness.

At first, only a few twinkling lights appeared in the

velvety darkness across the valley. But all at once, scores of windows were awakened across the plain and in the tiny neighbouring village of Bonnieux. It was as though a fairy world of make-believe had sprung to sparkling life at their feet. She sighed, resting her elbows on the table to cup her chin in her hands and turned her eyes to the east. A tiny sliver of silver had peeked over the darkened hill.

Silently, she caught Eddie's attention and pointed to it, sure that prosaic words would have lessened the moment of discovery. His eyes widened and he flashed her a grin as they both watched the moon rise above the treeline and float into the clear, cobalt sky.

"*Charmant, n'est-ce pas?*" she whispered, afraid to break the spell.

"*Oui*," Eddie said with matching reverence.

Her eyes swivelled to him in surprise. Did he know what she'd said?

His face split in two with a wide grin as though he'd told her a great joke. "No," he answered her unspoken question. "I don't know what you said, not exactly. But I'm sure you were remarking on how beautiful the evening is and on the romantic glow of the moon. Yes?"

She nodded. "Something like that, yes."

"And I agreed. It's a real special spot you've brought us to. Thanks." His eyes sought hers under the canopy of mini lights that were strung in glittering rows among the vines over their heads.

At that moment, their food arrived, along with a basket of fresh bread and two glasses of chilled white wine. The ambience was perfection itself. Except for some reason Elyse couldn't put her finger on, the feeling was not quite the same as the last time she'd been here. She smoothed the napkin on her lap. What was so different? The beauty of

Lacoste and the Luberon were the same. The food, the restaurant, and the shimmering moon set in a midnight blue sky were perfection itself. Her brow wrinkled with concentration.

"The food's delicious," Eddie broke into her thoughts. "You should dig in before yours gets cold." He took a bite and waved a hand at her plate as he chewed. He peered over the balcony, and she studied his face. The chiseled angles of his face were ruggedly handsome in the glowing light and her heart did a little flip.

He was right. Elyse looked at the curls of creamy parmesan that dotted her dish and grasped her fork. She pushed aside her misgivings and speared a tender dumpling of gnocchi. Soon, her plate was almost empty.

But it was not so easy to remove that odd feeling that hung over her, nor could she erase the memory of Armand sitting across from her at this same table. The man whose simple, caring friendship had left an indelible mark on her life.

Chapter Ten

Elyse rolled over and yanked the thin white coverlet up around her ears. She stared at the ceiling, humming the song Eddie had sung to her on the drive home last night. Apparently, it was called, "When You Say Nothing at All," but she'd never heard it before. She would never forget it now.

She and Eddie had shared some fabulous moments. His voice had serenaded her in the stillness of the car as the headlights picked out the twisty, tree-lined trail for home. It was one of the most romantic things that had ever happened to her. And then he'd said the sweetest things. She hugged herself with happiness, then squeezed her eyes shut and settled back on the pillow to go over his words in her mind—again. He was such a lovely man. How could she be so lucky?

"I ain't never met a woman like you, Elyse," he'd whispered, after softly crooning the love song. "Maybe I shouldn't be talkin' like this, so soon and all, but you have captured my heart. I feel like a better man just bein' with you."

He shuffled around in his seat, and she knew he was looking at her even though she couldn't see his face. Suddenly, it was hard to breathe. Her heart pounded so loudly in her ears, it almost drowned out his voice. But no, even now she could recall every inflection, every subtle nuance, and tone in his deeply resonant voice as he'd spoken wonderful words of love.

"Not sure how many days I have left on this good earth, but I knew the minute I clapped eyes on you that I wanted to spend 'em all at your side. You're perfect. We're perfect—together." Eddie took a deep, ragged breath and continued.

"I've been lookin' for you my whole life, Elyse. And if I died tomorrow, I'd be a happy man just because I got to spend the last few days of my life in your presence. That may sound hard to believe, but I'm speakin' straight from my heart." He shuffled again and spoke close to her ear. "I have a secret. I pleaded with my boss to let me come back here. I really liked you last year, but I was too scared to tell you. Now…" he paused for long moments. "Now, I've fallen for you—hard."

Elyse hadn't known what to say. Something held her back from saying the words that formed on the tip of her tongue. So, instead of saying anything she'd pulled the car over and kissed him…on the edge of the road…with her hazard lights casting a rhythmic red light over their upturned faces…she'd kissed him with all her heart.

What a night.

After she caught her breath, Elyse found the words she'd wanted to say.

"Eddie, per'aps I could 'elp you buy that 'ouse you spoke about. The one for you and your daughter to reunite in. If it's 'ard for you to come up with the money right now, maybe you could pay me back when you disperse your assets. It is important that you make amends with your daughter."

"Are you sure about that?" he'd asked, pulling her roughly into his arms all over again. "I don't want you to take any risks with your company, or your money. It's me that should be doing that."

"I think so," she said. Her thoughts churned. Should she do this thing? She, of course, had her own money, and didn't need to take from the business, or even inform her sons of such a decision. But was it the right thing to do? It certainly was a lot of money to give to someone she hadn't known for very long. It was Eddie though. Her nerves relaxed as she looked at his chiseled features. She felt an urge to cup his face in her hands and kiss him.

"I'm sure." But that was all she'd been allowed to say before he claimed her lips once more.

It had been well after ten o'clock when they finally arrived at Chateau de Belliveau. They tiptoed into the house like a couple of errant teenagers, giggling and trying so hard to be quiet in the dim light of the hallway that Eddie had backed into a table and knocked over a crystal candy dish. The laughter had, quite literally, come to a crashing halt after that, but they were still in high spirits even after the broken shards had been swept up and disposed of.

Arm-in-arm they'd climbed the winding staircase to their separate bedrooms and wished one another *bonne nuit* after one last lingering kiss.

It had been idyllic.

Elyse snapped out of her reverie as the alarm on her bedside table burst to life. She rolled over and clicked it off, rising to stretch and pad barefoot to the window in her short, lemon-yellow nightgown. Squinting past the curtains into the bright morning sunshine, she predicted another fabulous day ahead. She knew just what to do with it.

First though, she was anxious to see baby Celeste. Hurriedly, she showered and blow-dried her hair, then dressed in pale blue capris and a short-sleeved cotton top with poufy sleeves and a ruffled neckline. After applying a light smear of gloss to her lips, some sunscreen, mascara, and putting on her prettiest pair of gold, teardrop earrings, she stepped back from the mirror with satisfaction. Falling in love added a glow to her face that was hard to miss. She chuckled to herself as she slipped on her gold sandals, spun out the door, and flew down the stairs faster than her fifty-six years would usually allow.

Voices floated up to her. They emanated from the patio, and she revised her course, which had targeted the kitchen and her usual *café au lait*. Now she aimed for the big glass doors that led outside.

Before she could get there, a baby's cry pierced the air. Elyse sidestepped as Angelina, carrying a wailing Celeste, barreled through the open doors.

"*Désolé, maman,*" Angelina said in a terse voice as she headed for the staircase. "Celeste is wet. Soaked through. I'll be back in a minute."

Elyse chuckled. She remembered those times well and rather fondly, as it happened. The best times in life were when your children were young—or if lucky, when you fell, unexpectedly, rapturously in love.

She reached the opening and stood on the threshold, her eyes adjusting to the brilliant light of a cloudless Provencal sky. A young woman, tall and slender, but with curves in all the right places was poised at the edge of the pool in the tiniest beige bikini Elyse had ever seen—or not seen, she thought. She squinted hard to make sure the girl had anything on at all. Raphaël stood beside the girl, holding a large straw hat looking earnestly into her face as he appeared to plead with her. Eddie sat at the table looking shell-shocked, and Armand was pulling weeds in the herb beds with his back to the group.

The young woman let out a mock shriek of fear. Elyse stepped forward, trying to understand what was happening. But seemingly out of nowhere, Julien brushed past her with his mouth set in a straight line and eyes glaring.

"I'd stay away if I were you," he hissed.

"What's the matter?" she called to her eldest son, but he only lifted his coffee cup in a silent salute.

"*Bonne chance*," he called over his shoulder, disappearing around the corner.

She called to Raphaël. He jumped like he'd been struck with a hot poker. Whirling around, he tossed the hat onto the table, and rushed, red-faced to her side.

"Good morning, mother," he said loudly, leaning in to plant a kiss on both of her cheeks. Taking the opportunity of proximity, he mumbled in her ear. "This woman is as impossible as she is beautiful."

Elyse looked at him with dismay. 'This woman' must be their latest houseguest. Aware that Raphaël was also beating a hasty retreat, just like his brother, she looked at the willowy blonde bombshell who turned to her, a disdainful expression on her beautiful face.

"*Bonjour*," the young woman said, her features as vacant as her eyes. She looked at Elyse as though she'd been forced to welcome an unwanted visitor to *her* home.

"*Bonjour*. You must be Marie's granddaughter?" Elyse strode forward. The young woman inclined her head, long golden hair swishing forward over her face. She flicked it away with a practised hand.

"*Oui*, that is correct. I am Genevieve. And who are you?" Without waiting for an answer, Genevieve turned her back to Elyse, walking to the large glass table to retrieve the hat that Raphaël had tossed there. "I would like sunscreen and an espresso to be brought to me immediately," she ordered, pulling the hat down low and reaching for a package of cigarettes. She flicked open a lighter and the tip sizzled with flame. Genevieve threw back her head and took a long drag.

Mesmerized, Elyse watched as the young woman tapped ashes onto the patio and lowered herself gracefully onto one of the lounge chairs. She crossed long legs and continued speaking as though Elyse would be hanging on her every word. In fact, Elyse was, but not in the way that Genevieve might have thought.

The young woman behaved as though this were her personal spa. "It is imperative that I avoid the sun. Flawless skin is my number one asset." She leaned back in the shade, drumming the arm of her chair with long, pink fingernails and regarded Elyse from beneath a heavy fringe of false eyelashes. "Perhaps flawless skin 'as never mattered to you…whoever you are…but I can assure you it is critical to my continued success."

Elyse stiffened. "My name is Madame Belliveau," she ground out. "This is my 'ome and apparently…" she paused for emphasis, "you are my *guest*. Where is your grandmother?" Elyse had never formed a dislike for anyone so quickly. She swallowed all further remarks and turned toward Eddie. He'd disappeared. Smart man.

Genevieve waved an indolent hand, gesturing to the smaller, side door that led from the herb garden into the kitchen. She picked up a glossy magazine and began to leaf through it.

Balling her hands into fists, Elyse marched back through the house. She kept a sharp eye out for Armand, but didn't expect to see him, Eddie, or any of her family as she fumed her way to the kitchen.

She came to a halt beside the long marble-topped counter that ran almost the entire length of the room. Marie washed dishes at the sink.

"Good morning, Madame Laurent," Elyse said in clipped French. "I would like to speak with you."

The woman's shoulders hunched in her severe black dress, as though a karate chop had just been delivered to the back of her neck. She reached for a towel and, wiping her hands, slowly swung about, her face impassive with her hair scraped into a grey knot.

"You've met Genevieve?" It was more of a statement of fact than a question. Clearly Marie had anticipated this problem.

Elyse saw no reason to mince words. She hadn't helped to run a successful business for thirty-five years without managing a few difficult people. The most upsetting part was the young woman's entitled attitude. It was intolerable.

"Yes," she said, narrowing her eyes. "Within thirty seconds of meeting your granddaughter I was ordered to bring her an espresso and a bottle of sunscreen. Perhaps you would like to fetch those items for her, because I will not."

Elyse was beyond irritated and waited for Marie's response.

The chef twisted the towel between her hands, her face anguished.

"I feel terrible about this," she said.

Elyse shook her head in bewilderment. "You do?"

"I haven't seen Genevieve for two years. Not since she left for Paris to become a model." Marie plopped down on a chair, rolling and unrolling the towel. "I had no idea she'd become a spoiled, self-centered brat."

Elyse dropped into the chair next to her chef. Could this really be the Marie who had waltzed in here two days ago looking like a thundercloud?

"What can we do about it?" Elyse asked. She folded her hands in her lap and waited.

"She is my problem," Marie answered at length. "I'm not sorry she came to visit me. Maybe I could have a positive effect in her life. For sure I can knock her off that high horse she's sitting on to start." Marie's dark brown eyes took on a steely glint. "I'm just sorry I brought her here. Perhaps you should start looking for someone to replace me right away. Then I could take Genevieve home where she belongs. Remind her of her roots, so to speak." Marie shot Elyse a grim smile.

"Nonsense!" Elyse heard herself exclaim. "That is to say if you want to leave you should feel free to go. I can easily manage meals on my own. But if you wish to stay, and you are prepared to take a stand, well, we can make it work."

Marie eyed her doubtfully. "You are sure?"

Elyse sat back in her chair. She needed a coffee. This was the second time in twelve hours she'd been asked that question. They were life-altering questions that required careful thought, at least in the short-term. But she gave the same answer as last time.

"Yes," she said without a trace of indecision. "I'm positive."

"Good. I appreciate this. And you must put her in her place as well. I insist." Marie sent Elyse a shy smile. Then she rose from her seat and folded the mangled towel with great deliberation. "No time like the present, I always say. Excuse me." With a slight bow of her head, the sturdy little woman strode to the door leading out to the garden and closed it behind her with a firm *click*.

Elyse smiled to herself and moved to the coffee maker. It only took a few minutes to make her favourite beverage, and cradling it between her hands she took a sip of the aromatic brew. *Yes, that was better.*

Catching sight of Armand's moss green t-shirt in the garden, Elyse took her cup and walked outside. He must have collected Genevieve from the train this morning and brought her directly here.

"Good morning," she said, coming up behind him as he squatted beside a clump of thyme, pulling weeds. "It's good to see you."

"Is it?' he asked, straightening. His eyes bored into hers. She knew there was a wealth of meaning in those two simple words, but she didn't want to become embroiled in what was now the past.

"Yes," she said lightly. "Why didn't you tell me it was your aunt who was taking your place?"

He shrugged. "She was between jobs, available, and is the best cook around. She taught me everything I know."

"That's what she said too." Elyse smiled at him, hoping to elicit a similar response.

He relaxed a little. "I'm sure she did." He rubbed dirt off his hands and craned his neck to peer over the shrubbery toward the pool. The sound of raised voices floated to them on a warm breeze from that direction. "Sounds like Marie is having a few words with Genevieve."

"I hope so." Elyse said nothing more. It was not her place to criticize Armand's family. A few days ago, she would have discussed the situation with him before anyone else. There was nothing she couldn't have said to this man. But now—now there was so much tension between them. She had hurt him and there was no going back to what they once had. Her heart clenched with sadness, and she turned away.

"It truly is nice to see you, Armand," she said in a voice barely audible to her own ears. "I've missed you."

A hand snaked out and caught her wrist, whirling her around and into his arms before she could say a word of protest. He folded her into him, molding every single curve of her body to his as though he might never have the chance again. She heard his sharp intake of breath at her ear and then he was gone. He pulled away, letting her go as suddenly as he'd held her and strode down the garden path without another word.

She found herself near to tears. What was happening to her? She raised a hand to her brow. She needed to find Angelina and Celeste, then bury herself in baby snuggles. It was a remedy to all ailments. Besides, she hadn't seen nearly enough of her granddaughter. Elyse imagined her sons had gone to work and Eddie, wherever he was, could wait.

As she passed through the dining room, she noticed that Marie had discreetly closed the double patio doors. The older woman stood, waving her arms in front of Genevieve, her voice seeping through the walls. The tirade appeared to be without end and Elyse almost felt sorry for the girl.

But not quite.

Hurrying upstairs, Elyse thought of all the changes that had been wrought at the chateau in the last few days, Celeste was the very best one. She turned down the hallway to Julien and Angelina's private apartment and tapped on the door.

"*Entrez*," Angelina called.

Elyse let herself in and walked down another, narrower hallway to the room she had helped Angelina decorate for the baby.

Done in an Old World style, the nursery was large and airy with long white drapes at each of the two windows and an old-fashioned, white-ruffled crib gracing center stage. A two-toned palette of powder blue and white created a soft, dreamy, cloud-like space that offered tranquility and peace. A wallpaper mural, that Angelina and Elyse had cursed as they struggled to put it up, but loved once it was done, covered one whole wall. It depicted a gentle woodland scene, painted as an artist might have done in the 1700s.

A toy box, also white with blue trim, sat empty—for now, and two large bureaus, one with a round mirror over-top, were filled to the brim with cute little outfits. A huge bouquet of blue and purple hydrangeas and a fringed lamp sat on a small round table beside a cozy armchair with a matching cushiony footstool. Even the floor was covered with a striped blue and white rug.

Angelina was just scooping Celeste off the changing table where she'd been cleaned and swapped into a fresh pink romper.

"Would you hold her while I take care of the wet clothes," Angelina asked, kissing her little daughter on her chubby cheeks.

"I would love to." Elyse held out her arms and snuggled the sweet-scented baby to her heart. "I would 'old this little darling until she was twenty-five years old if I could." She laughed, seating herself in the comfy chair to bounce Celeste on her knee. The baby cooed and flapped her tiny arms.

"So, how's the tour guide thing going?" asked Angelina

as she tidied up. "Have you shown Eddie more of your favourite places?"

"I 'ave." Elyse decided not to say more. She wasn't trying to be evasive, but her relationship with Eddie was so fresh and new. She wanted to keep it quiet for a while, until she got used to it herself. It had nothing to do with Armand, she told herself with conviction.

"It's nice to 'ave a willing subject," she said. "And 'e seems to enjoy our excursions."

"Did you see Armand?" Angelina's question dropped into the room like a bomb. "He's around here somewhere this morning. I think he brought Marie's granddaughter."

Elyse buried her face in the crook of Celeste's neck and kissed her. How to answer? Yes, she'd seen him alright. He'd just clung to her like his life depended on it. Meanwhile, she'd fallen for someone else. It all felt incredibly fickle, even to her. Yet she had to answer the uncomfortable question.

"I saw 'im just a moment ago," she said finally. "I thought 'e seemed fine."

Angelina came to stand in front of her, a basket of laundry in her hands. "I didn't mean to bring up a painful subject. I just care about you—and him too."

"I know," Elyse shrugged with a sigh. "I confess I think about 'im often. But I cannot create feelings where there are none."

"No, of course not," Angelina looked at her shrewdly, as though she didn't quite believe what Elyse was saying. "Anyway, if you want to visit with Celeste for about an hour, I have some clothes to wash."

Elyse leaned back in the chair and picked up a rattle from the table. "That would be perfect," she said. "I thought I would take Eddie to see Roussillon today. If 'e doesn't 'ave other plans. But first I want to spend time with my little sweetheart."

It was an enjoyable visit for both of them. Celeste fell asleep in Elyse's arms, and she laid the baby in her crib and covered her with a light sheet before closing the curtains near her crib. Angelina arrived moments later to declare she would take a much-needed nap while the baby slept. Neither of them mentioned the arrival of Genevieve.

Elyse slipped out the door and made her way to the east wing of the house, then to her own rooms. She refreshed her lip gloss and grabbed her purse. It was time to look for Eddie and ask him whether he was available to go on another jaunt.

She found him in the salon, standing with arms folded behind his back at the windows, a worried expression on his face. When he saw her, he threw his arms wide and grinned.

"There you are," he said, folding her into his embrace.

"Did you 'ave breakfast?" she asked, pulling back. She peered over his shoulder, hoping Armand had left.

"Marie gave me a fresh croissant and some coffee, yes." He turned to check where she'd been looking with a puzzled frown. "Is something wrong?" he asked.

She shook her head and averted her gaze.

"You look happy," he said. "And I don't imagine it's from spending time with your new houseguest."

Elyse laughed. "You're right. But I think Marie will be good for the girl. And per'aps I will 'ave some input too." She moved to the sofa and plumped a cushion. "I am wondering if you 'ave 'eard from the police or the United States embassy about your passport?" She looked up expectantly.

"No," he said, the creases on his forehead growing deeper. "I haven't heard a thing. Although I called my company back in the US, and the number I was given at the embassy. Apparently, my new passport is on its way. Guess these things take time."

"*Je m'en fiche*," she said, waving a hand. "It doesn't matter. I don't care 'ow long it takes because I am 'appy you are 'ere. And what about," she lowered her voice to a whisper, "the property...Will you make an offer? Should we go to see it?"

"Hold on," Eddie said, holding up his hands against the barrage of questions. "I need to make a decision on that, yes, but not today. I'd much rather be with you and not worry about it today."

"Perfect," she said happily. "I 'ave chosen somewhere for us to go that I think you will enjoy."

Within half an hour they were on the road and winging along the A7 to Cavaillon.

"We cannot take the same route every time," Elyse explained as she manoeuvred through yet another roundabout. "I want you to see Roussillon. The landscape is so unusual."

"Well, you haven't let me down yet." Eddie twisted in his seat to look at her. "In so many ways." He shot her a meaningful grin and she giggled.

"Be serious," she demanded. "And you didn't tell me much about the property you want to buy. I'd like to 'ear about it."

"Let's see." He said, settling back in his seat. "I've only seen pictures, mind you, but it's pretty as a picture from what I could tell. There's about twenty acres devoted to an olive grove, and a house set back from the road down a winding lane bordered by plane trees. The house is small, only two bedrooms, and it needs some work, but I ain't afraid of hard work," he boasted. Eddie gripped his knees and leaned forward. "I'd welcome it. First place I would have ever owned. Course there'll be some logistics to figure out with movin' to France, but people do it every year. Right?"

"*Mais oui*," Elyse agreed. "You can do it. You 'ave never owned a 'ome of your own?"

"Nope," he said regretfully. "I was always moving around the country for work. Dragged my family with me too. It wasn't good for any of us."

"What was your wife's name? You said she died, how did it 'appen?"

Eddie stared out the window at the passing scenery for long moments before he answered. "Her name was Kathy. We'd gone to high school together and kept dating even when she went away to college. Her family didn't approve of me 'cause, like I said, my father drank too much and always figured he'd make it big in Nashville as a country/western singer. So, my family was poor, and I had to work two or three jobs at the same time to keep a roof over our heads." He swivelled in his seat to stare at her. "You sure you wanna hear all this. It's kinda depressin'."

"Yes," she said softly. "I want to know all about you, Eddie."

"Okay. Anyway, Kathy and I ran off and got married before she finished college. That was a mistake. I shouldn't have let her do that, but we were young and in love. We were poor, but happy. Then, I found a good job with the railroad and stuck with that for about fifteen years, and she worked in a senior citizen's home. Kathy was real kind to folks." Eddie paused. "Those people loved her. After a few years, we had our little girl, Angie and the first six years of her life were perfect." He stopped and wiped a hand across his eyes.

"Jeez, tellin' this story is gonna make me cry," he said in a shaky voice. "And I hate cryin'!" He took a deep breath and continued. "That's when Kathy started to feel sick. But she was no complainer. She refused to see a doctor until she was in too much pain to go on. The doc told us it was the final stages of pancreatic cancer. She was given three months, if she was lucky, but she made it three years."

"I am so very sorry," Elyse didn't know what to say. She shouldn't have asked him about his wife, though it had seemed a reasonable question, if she truly cared about him and he cared for her. He'd heard all about how Georges had died in a car accident the year before when he visited.

"Thanks. It makes me sad, mostly for what could have been, and of course for our daughter who grew up without her mother. The years when I was alone with Angie were hard, but good. It was…when I had to leave unexpectedly that she turned against me. Ain't seen her much since."

This was a heavy topic indeed. Elyse reached across the console and squeezed his hand. "You'll make it all up to 'er," she said. "When we get you that 'ouse and you are able to give 'er a place to come spend time with you. What does she do now? Could she take time to spend 'ere?"

"I know she could," he said. "She's a schoolteacher and has the summer off as well as two weeks at Christmas. I tracked her down just before I left for France. If she's willin', I just need to finalize the deal."

He reached for her hand and leaned close. "Do you mind if I ask you a personal question?" he asked, then continued, not waiting for her answer. "Would you ever get married again?" He looked at her intently, one thumb tracing lazy circles on the palm of her hand.

"I—I suppose," she stammered. "Per'aps. I 'aven't thought about it. Why would you ask such a thing?" She pulled her hand back with a smile of apology and kept it on the wheel. His daring made her blush and respond with her own bold query. Yes, she had gotten to know him last summer, and their relationship was progressing quickly. But surely, he couldn't be talking about the two of *them*.

He had the grace to look abashed. "Sorry, Elyse. I can see I've made you uncomfortable and I apologize. I just figure, at our age, why waste time. I'm sixty, by the way, but I won't ask you. No lady likes to reveal her age."

He had turned the discussion back to a lighter vein and she was grateful. Things were happening at an alarming rate, she realized with a jolt.

She'd spent more than a year grieving for her late husband, and now two wonderful men were interested in her at the same time. One of them was the closest friend she'd ever had, but had lost, possibly forever. And the other needed a substantial loan and was talking about marriage! It was more than a little overwhelming.

Chapter Eleven

"The soil seems to be getting' awful red," Eddie remarked, leaning against his seatbelt as they slowed and drove up a street marked on either side by beautiful homes in various hues of oranges and reds. "Is this it?"

"*Oui*." Elyse felt pleased. She'd managed to find several of her favourite spots without needing a map, or GPS. For a woman who had only gotten her driving license a few months ago, she was doing quite well. They rolled into the village. Visitors lined the sidewalks as businesses spilled onto the street to display their wares. A banner floated across the street overhead, announcing that this was a '*Village français préféré*' or a favourite French village. And it was.

They broke free of the tall buildings and the landscape fell away from a low stone wall on their right. She looked to the left, hoping there would be a place for her to park and spotted a car pulling out to leave. Perfect.

Eddie gave a low whistle. "This is gorgeous," he said. "A little like Sedona, in Arizona, but with a French flair. I love it!"

She cast him a quick glance, her heart quickening at his pleasure. Elyse parked and, after each of them donned their hats and sunglasses, they got out of the car. The heat hit Elyse like a blast furnace. It always happened like that after spending a prolonged period of time in air-conditioning, but she was accustomed to it. Eddie didn't miss a beat.

He held out his arm as usual and she slid her own arm inside. He pressed her close to him as they headed for the gap between buildings where one could view the valley beyond and the ochre cliffs.

The colours were marvellous. All exposed earth was a gorgeous shade of burnt orange, set off to advantage by the deep green of the forest below the town. Time and weather had worn away a cliff directly to their right, and she admired its carved angles as they sat on the stone wall posing for pictures. Eddie held her close, one arm slung possessively around her waist as they posed for a selfie.

"Again, you've brought me to a wonderful destination," he said, taking off his hat and wiping an arm across his brow. "Let's wander around, shall we?"

"Roussillon is situated in one of the largest deposits of ochre in the world," she said, never quite able to leave the tour guide side of her at home.

Linking arms, they strolled along, passing lavender shops, clothing, baskets, and ice cream for sale. People were indulging in all of it. Parcels and bags hung from their arms and a mixture of languages washed over Elyse as they passed groups of holidaymakers from all over the world.

The road became steep, and they turned to the left down a narrow lane where cars were forbidden to go. It was shady and Eddie took off his clip-on sunglasses to polish them. A few minutes of steady climbing, and they emerged into a pedestrian square surrounded by three-story red buildings with the ubiquitous blue Provencal shutters closed against the blazing sun.

Turning, they followed a little lane farther up the hill where trailing vines tumbled over the multi-coloured red rock walls, while cedars and olive trees appeared to spring from the rocks themselves. Around each turn was something else to see—a bush covered in ruby red azaleas, a church hidden among the houses, a tower with tiny steps precariously leading up a ledge to the bell suspended at the top—all picture-perfect places. They paused many times to snap photos of themselves and of the scenery.

Finally, they reached the very pinnacle of the village where a gentle breeze blew her hair, and the panoramic view surrounded them. Eddie gathered her into his arms and tucked a stray lock of hair behind her ear before stooping to place a delicate kiss on her lips.

"Marry me," he said softly. "And I'll spend the rest of my life making you happy and showing you how much you're loved."

Elyse melted into him. It felt right. All the longings she'd had over the last year, the hopes she'd not dared dream were being realized. Why shouldn't she take a chance? Why not grab a piece of the happiness she'd missed since being alone? It seemed the most natural thing to do to agree, but something held her back from uttering the words. Her heart felt conflicted, to say the least.

His eyes gleamed only centimeters from her own and she felt as though she were drowning in their depths. Then, as though sensing her reticence, his arms slid away, and he took her hand and raised it to his lips.

"Answer me when you feel comfortable," he said. "I would never push you." Together they stepped to the edge of the paved plateau above the village and looked out on the Luberon in all its beauty. "Come," he said, tugging at her arm. "Let's go explore."

They wandered the streets of Roussillon for the rest of the afternoon, poking through tiny eclectic shops, stopping for a glass of wine overlooking the valley, and choosing their favourite flavours of ice cream to eat in the shade of the old buildings. It was another lovely day, but Elyse wanted to be back in time for dinner. So, they left town as shadows lengthened against the buildings, and headed for home.

It was an enjoyable drive spent discussing the sights they'd seen over the past three days. Eddie didn't ask any more difficult questions and Elyse relaxed. Just before five, they pulled into the driveway and stopped behind a small blue Peugeot.

She caught her breath, knowing who owned the car—Armand. Elyse felt torn between reversing and driving away to hide until he left or running inside to greet him with joy. She couldn't explain her feelings anymore. Not even to herself. She felt pulled in two directions. Her world was far too confusing lately. However, the decision was taken out of her hands as Eddie reached for the door, muttering under his breath.

"I swear, if it's that damned ex-butler or cook or whatever the hell he is, I'm gonna order him to get out." His face looked grim and determined as his left hand clenched into a fist.

Elyse was alarmed. She laid a restraining hand on Eddie's arm. "You 'ave no right to tell 'im anything of the sort," she said levelly. "This is my 'ome and Armand is my friend. There must be a reason 'e 'as returned, but that is not for you to question." Irritation rose in Elyse as she looked at the man seated next to her. Did she really know him at all? What right did he have to order people about as though he owned the place?

Eddie slumped back in his seat, an apologetic grin spreading across his face. However, she got the sense he was only smoothing his anger over in order to appease her, not because he realized he was wrong.

And he *was* wrong.

"I'm sorry, honey," he said, patting her hand where it laid on his sleeve. "I got a little carried away. Please forgive me. Guess I feel protective…I believe that man likes you more than as a friend."

So…Elyse thought, even Eddie could see what she had missed for months. Armand did care for her. She sighed. Life was just too complicated. How she wished the last week had never happened, and things could go back to the way they'd been just before Celeste was born.

"Come," she said, not wanting to discuss it anymore. "Let's go inside."

Before they reached the bottom of the stairs leading to the front doors, Armand himself came around the corner. He was threading his way along the garden path with a large cardboard box in his arms.

"*Salut*," he said, giving them both a curt nod. "Please, don't let me stop you. I was just picking up a few recipe books."

"*Pas de problème*," Elyse responded, not even considering the English equivalent.

She couldn't help but notice what Armand was wearing. He had changed since this morning. When not working, he always dressed in casual clothes with an elegant style that was all his own. A white, short-sleeved button-up shirt was tucked into grey linen trousers, cuffed around his ankles, and light-coloured loafers graced his feet. Reflective sunglasses glinted in the sun as he walked toward them.

Armand didn't smile, nor did he show any sign of stopping, which was just as well, but as he drew closer to Elyse he pulled off the glasses and his eyes flicked over her face, his gaze softening. But then his jaw flexed, and he barely glanced at Eddie as he continued toward them.

"If you approve," Armand said, addressing Elyse, "I will return bright and early tomorrow so that Maria and I may begin to prepare for Celeste's party?"

"Of course." Elyse agreed quietly. "The celebration is Saturday, after all, so I am sure you will need plenty of time."

"*Bien.*" Armand drew level with them.

Eddie had stopped behind her, his feet crunching in the gravel as he stepped in front of Armand. Barring the path, he addressed him aggressively. "Maybe Elyse and I will have something big to celebrate ourselves, ain't that right honey?" he drawled, grabbing Elyse by the hand and tugging her toward him. "How are you at makin' weddin' cakes, Almond?"

Armand's eyes dropped to their entwined fingers. His eyes darkened with pain as they caught hers. Her chest constricted.

He looked at Eddie. Elyse watched with a sick feeling in the pit of her stomach as the two men she cared about most in the world, apart from her sons, glared at one another in a measuring way.

She felt a wave of heat suffuse her body. Tugging her hand away from Eddie's, she applied both of them to her reddened cheeks. She opened her mouth to speak, but words would not come. This was horrible. Eddie was baiting him, laying some sort of claim to her and, as an added dig, purposely mispronounced Armand's name.

Armand detoured onto the lawn, skirted a flower bed, and calmly caught the path once more before he responded. "If Elyse asked me to make 'er a wedding cake, I would make the finest one in all the land," he said. "But for you," he flung over his shoulder, "I would not even boil water."

"Why you…" Eddie started toward Armand, but Elyse snaked an arm out and caught his shirt sleeve. She believed Eddie would have struck Armand at that moment. It was as though a heavy curtain had just been drawn from her eyes and she saw clearly for the first time in months.

"Leave 'im alone!" she commanded. Really, this was almost like two boys fighting in the schoolyard. Over her!

Armand slid his glasses back into place. Then Elyse watched as he placed the box in the back seat of his car, hopped in, and spun out of the driveway. Suddenly, she felt weary and longed to escape to her private rooms. "I 'ave a 'eadache and believe I shall lie down for a while," she told Eddie. "Please tell anyone who asks that I will be down in an 'our."

She lifted the back of a hand to her overheated brow. Managing a faint smile, she said. "It was a lovely day. I will see you at dinner."

Eddie's face creased in a frown of what she assumed was concern, but she left him standing there and hurried up the steps. Escaping into the coolness of the chateau, she felt grateful she had somewhere to hide.

Above all, she desired time to herself to think. This final exchange between the two men, for some reason, had spoken to her louder than all the words that had been uttered. It was as though a candle had been lit inside her soul, illuminating the havoc within. Her head and her heart, were in turmoil.

She scurried up to her room and locked the door behind her as she collapsed against it, breathing a sigh of relief. She kicked off her sandals and laid on her bed for nearly an hour, staring at the ceiling and trying to rest her mind. It didn't help. Finally, she arose, showered off the dust of the day, and changed into an orange dress with navy polka-dots and full skirt that belted at the waist.

Her stomach rumbled. Looking at the clock on her bedside table, she realized it was time for dinner. Although she would much rather have eaten alone, and perhaps slipped in to see Celeste before bed, she knew she needed to speak with their house guest. At least one of her problems was solved.

She could not now, or ever, marry Edward Wright.

Sliding into a pair of strappy black sandals, she made her way downstairs to the salon where she heard voices and laughter echoing through the house. Just as she was about to enter, Eddie strode out. Seeing her, he slid an arm around her shoulders and directed her away.

"Dinner is going to be about half an hour more," he said. "Would you walk with me in the garden you love so much?"

"*Bien sûr.*" She answered calmly, but her insides tensed, and her throat was in danger of closing off. *Eddie would have to be told sometime*, she reasoned. Why not now? As Marie had said, 'There's no time like the present.'

She led the way through to the patio rather than bothering Marie in the kitchen. From there she walked down the path leading to the herb beds and then onto the main path. Elyse took a deep breath. The tangy scent of the cedars floated to her on the evening breeze and the nodding blooms of her flowers gave her courage.

She breathed deep, the soft perfume pulling her into a memory of Armand. She and Armand had spent a lot of time wandering through this garden over the past year. No. She wouldn't allow thoughts of him to interfere now. She needed to speak to Eddie with a clear mind.

Eddie caught up and reached for her, but she anticipated his move and cleverly avoided him. She pointed to the bench that Julien had erected for her beneath a bower of wisteria. The purple blooms had gone now, but the greenery still draped over the seat to create a hidden nook.

"Let's sit," she said with a smile. Dropping his arm to his side, he cast her a reproachful look. He was clearly upset that she hadn't taken his proffered hand, but Elyse couldn't worry about that now. "It's beautiful out 'ere, *n'est-ce pas*?"

"Yes," he answered doubtfully. "But I get the feeling you want to tell me something important. Is it about the money you've promised me? We can draw up legal paperwork, you know. Make it official and binding. You have my word that I'll pay you back. Even when we're married."

Eddie sat on the polished wooden seat beside her and gazed into her face, his eyes dark and brooding with a frown of concern digging deep furrows into his forehead. She remained silent. "You *will* marry me, won't you Elyse?"

She sighed. "I cannot marry you Eddie," she said gently. "This relationship we started is moving far too fast for me. I —I care about you and I 'ave fun with you, but that is not enough reason to marry someone. We need time to be sure of what we have and—"

"It's that chef isn't it!" he broke in angrily. "That Almond guy with the nice car and smooth words. Are you in love with him?" She sensed Eddie was struggling to hold his disappointment in check, but how long would that last.

Elyse had envisioned this going much differently. Still, she tried to be patient and honest. "Armand 'as been my best friend for many years," she said simply, twisting the belt of her dress. "My friendship with 'im 'as nothing to do with us, and I will not discuss it with you."

"Oh...I think it does, but you're right," he said with a sigh, leaning forward and surrendering in a gentle voice. He then dropped his head into his hands. "I've pushed you and rushed our relationship. Sorry, Elyse. I just can't leave a good thing alone to grow naturally." He straightened, his face pleading. "Can you forgive me? Maybe we could go back to just being friends?"

"*Oui*," she said unsteadily. "We *are* friends. Now, 'ow about we go back inside and 'ave dinner and a good night's sleep. Everything will look better in the morning." Rising, she gestured that he follow her. "Per'aps your passport and credit cards will arrive. One never knows the surprises that are waiting around the corner." She forced herself to smile and led the way back inside.

"Truer words were never spoken," Eddie said cryptically.

The aroma of seafood greeted them at the door, and she ushered him into the dining room where her family waited. Even a much subdued Genevieve had joined them in a glittering sequin dress. They seated themselves and a beaming Marie plunked steaming bowls of food and a selection of cold salads onto the table.

Elyse could hardly wait for the meal to be over, so she could retire to her room once more. Conversations flowed over her head. No one noticed her silence as mechanically she spooned tiny portions of food onto her plate and pushed them back and forth.

Her mind was spinning. Life felt out of control. She couldn't eat, although she was hungry, and the food looked delicious. Had she encouraged Eddie enough that he truly believed she would marry him after only a few days of being together? He had asked her, to be sure. What shocked her was that she had actually toyed with the idea if only for a short bit. That was the bizarre part. Yet, even in those moments, she had known, deep down, that she could not truly love this man—let alone marry him. Perhaps she was only in love with the *idea* of a second chance at marriage and happiness.

It was all too much. Folding her napkin, she laid it on the table and excused herself, citing the headache she'd mentioned earlier.

"Thank you for a wonderful meal, Marie," she said, holding a hand to her temple. She shoved her chair back. "Please excuse me." She bent to place a kiss on top of Celeste's head.

"You are welcome," the lady said graciously. "I will give Armand the recipes." She flung an arm wide and everyone at the table chuckled. All except Eddie, Elyse noticed. He glowered into his dessert.

He lifted a hand at the last moment to wave to her. "Sweet dreams," he called as she rounded the corner.

Elyse plodded to her room, grateful for the time alone. She needed to unravel the mess she'd unwittingly gotten herself into and hopefully without anyone else getting hurt. But the look in Armand's eyes today still haunted her.

Did she honestly have no feelings for him? She wasn't so sure anymore. But even if she did, it was too late.

He was gone.

Chapter Twelve

The sound of someone banging on the door awakened her. Blearily, Elyse rolled over and looked at the clock on her bedside table. She'd overslept! It was well after eleven in the morning, and she was still lolling about in bed. She hadn't lain in bed like this since she was a teenager.

Unable to sleep the night before, she'd paced the floors, tossed back and forth in bed, and finally sat up reading a book till almost 5am. Then, in desperation, she'd resorted to one of the sleeping pills the doctor had prescribed after Georges' death. *It hadn't been a good idea*, she thought groggily.

The hammering sound came again, followed by the door handle rattling.

"*Maman, tu vas bien?*" Julien yelled from the hallway.

"*Oui, oui, je vais bien,*" she called. Elyse flipped the covers away and slid from her bed. She was a bit woozy from the pill. Somehow, she grabbed her dressing gown and belted it around her waist before unlatching the door and admitting her eldest son.

163

"I'm so sorry to worry you, sweetheart," she said, reaching up to place a hand on his cheek. It didn't matter how old her children were, they would always be her babies. "I couldn't sleep, so I took a tablet to force myself. I suppose it worked too well," she stifled a yawn.

Julien hugged her. "I'm glad you're alright. Angelina called me to come break the door down," he laughed. "She'd knocked every fifteen minutes for the past hour and was getting worried. Even Eddie was concerned." He hugged her close then bent to look into her face. "You're really okay?"

"Yes—yes, the pill was a mistake I won't repeat." Not wanting to discuss the reasons she hadn't been able to sleep, she went on, "And how is Celeste this morning?"

Julien's face creased into a grin. "She's so sweet," he enthused. "Being a father is the best job in the world." He stepped back to the doorway and winked. "I'll let you get ready for the day, mother. I think Eddie is rather anxious that you arise. He seems to have some plan or other."

"Oh," Elyse said in a small voice. "Did he by chance, receive any mail, or telephone calls from the United States about his passport and credit cards?"

"He had a phone call," Julien answered, stroking his jaw thoughtfully. "I heard his phone ring during breakfast, but he left the room to speak, so I have no idea what it was about." He waved to his mother. "I must get back to work. Love you," he called, and then he disappeared.

Acting on pure reflex, Elyse made her bed and then slumped onto it. Since her epiphany of the evening before, she thought it might be difficult to spend the whole day with Eddie. She wasn't sure what feelings she had toward either of the men who were jealous of each other and vying for her love, but she wasn't going to be rushed into anything.

With that, she lifted her chin and stood up. She would take Eddie for one last outing she had planned. Then she would explain why they could not continue to spend so much time together and send him to work with Julien and Raphaël for a few days. With luck, his passport would arrive during that time. As far as the money for his property went, well, she knew she'd been swept up in the moment when she'd promised her help. However, that would require further consideration. At this moment, she was not keen on lending him money of any sort. Exactly what her feelings were toward Eddie, she would try to sort out today.

Elyse selected an outfit and threw it onto a chair while she splashed cool water on her face, brushed her teeth, and applied her makeup. These daily rituals helped to wake her from the grogginess she felt.

The weather forecast predicted a hotter day than usual, so she'd chosen a loose, white shift dress with brown leather sandals and a chunky gold and crystal necklace. She clipped her hair into a bun at her nape and added red lipstick before throwing it into her bag along with her sunglasses and phone. She grabbed a matching hat and made her way downstairs. Coffee, that's what she needed.

As she passed the patio doors, she saw Genevieve reclined on the chaise lounge under an umbrella with a cell phone held to her ear. Elyse hurried past. The girl appeared to have been straightened out by her grandmother. Last night at dinner she'd barely said a word, but Elyse didn't feel like taking a chance on it.

She found Eddie in the kitchen at the small table beneath the floating staircase Elyse had designed. Again, he was reading a newspaper and sipping a coffee which he set down as she entered.

"*Bonjour*," she said brightly, smiling from him to Marie. Eddie whistled.

"You look mighty pretty today, darlin'," he said, looking her up and down. What a strange thing to say. She'd turned down his marriage proposal, so he should be experiencing hurt and perhaps rejection. Yet he acted as though nothing at all had happened the evening before.

Certainly, the compliment fell flat. She merely smiled and walked past him to make the usual *café au lait*, feeling uncomfortable.

Marie busily kneaded dough on the center island. She nodded her head in the direction of the espresso maker. "*Désolée*, Madame Belliveau," she said, lifting hands covered in flour to explain. "I cannot make it for you right now."

Elyse waved her apologies away. "I make myself coffee every day. And please, call me Elyse."

As she depressed the lever and a stream of steaming coffee trickled into her mug, she wondered, not for the first time, why Eddie was looking at a French newspaper. She glanced at him, sprawled back in his chair, leaning on the table to watch her with narrowed eyes. Something about him unnerved her today.

Yesterday he had professed his undying love for her. Surely, if it were genuine, he would not be looking at her as though she'd just poisoned his food.

"Julien tells me you would like to see more of the countryside," she said, deciding not to question it. Elyse seized a croissant from a bag and sat opposite him. She bit into it and chewed, cradling her mug and breathing in the steam. The rich aroma was heavenly.

Leaning on the table, and resting his chin on laced fingers, he searched her face. "That's right." His lifted a shoulder and let it drop. "If you don't mind, of course? Last night, after you went to bed, I heard from the United States passport services. I should have everything in place by tomorrow. So, maybe today is our last chance for sightseeing. Your big party is Saturday, right? I wouldn't want to interfere with that anyways."

Elyse thought she detected sarcasm rather than consideration in his tone, but he delivered it with a broad smile, and she forced herself to relax. This was Eddie. The man she'd fancied she was falling for. She reached out and touched his hand.

"Then we will go," she said, taking a sip of the fiery hot liquid. "I 'ave always wanted to take someone to see the *Grottes de Thouzon.*"

"And what's that?" Eddie asked leaning over to tie his sneaker. He wore jeans and a blue, long-sleeve button-up shirt, which seemed hot for the day, but she wasn't going to question his choices. He had to know by now what the heat was like. Pushing the hair from his forehead, he straightened and reached for her hand, lifting it to his lips.

Elyse flushed. Her back was to Marie, so she couldn't tell if the woman was watching. Yet this sudden display of affection made her uneasy, particularly in front of Armand's aunt.

"*Grotte* is French for cave, and it is the perfect place to go on a hot day," she said. "The system of caves was formed by an ancient underground river. You can see stalactites and stalagmites that took thousands of years to develop. The drive to reach it is lovely too."

"Will we pass by the cedar forest?"

Elyse was a little surprised by his question. "No," she said. "I thought we would take a more direct route."

Eddie finished the last drops of his coffee and set the cup down carefully. "I'd like to go to the cedar path first," he said, not meeting her eyes. "That walk meant a lot to me and if it's the last time I have an opportunity to go there, it would be great if we could repeat it. Would that be alright?" He looked up, his gaze unfathomable.

"*Bien sûr*," she said in French, feeling flustered. Eddie looked so intense. "Of course, we can stop there first and go for a walk if you wish."

"Great," he said, jumping to his feet and dusting crumbs from his legs. "Ready?"

It didn't take Elyse long to find her car keys. Though when she exited the front door with her hat and bag, Eddie was already in the passenger seat of her car. He certainly appeared anxious to leave.

For the first ten minutes they talked about the weather and how it was supposed to hit 38 degrees Celsius today. Then they thoroughly covered last night's meal and what a good cook Maria was. That led to a discussion concerning the about-face Genevieve had undergone. Elyse hadn't seen much of the young woman since their initial meeting, but Eddie assured her that the model was a new woman.

"I don't know what your chef said to her," he went on, "but her attitude improved right away. You'd already left the table last night, but she actually helped her grandmother clean up."

They lapsed into silence. Gone was the easy repartee of the last few days. They only spoke of the most mundane subjects now. Elyse knew it was last night's revelation that had caused it, but there was nothing else she could have done. That final confrontation between Armand and Eddie had opened her eyes to the facts. Eddie was volatile and marrying him would be a mistake. Her thoughts slipped back to the first incident where she'd noticed it. It had shocked her when he'd become so unreasonably angry with the teenagers who'd bumped him on the path. Not to mention the other situations. She'd been too quick to explain them away and make excuses for his behavior.

Not when it came to his animosity toward Armand, though. It was too much. Picking a fight with a man she respected and...and what...loved? It had been the next word to pop into her thoughts. But that couldn't be. He was her very good friend, but that was all. Wasn't it?

Eddie cleared his throat. "That's Lourmarin ahead, isn't it?" he asked.

Elyse had been so preoccupied, she hadn't noticed. Peering at the roundabout they were entering, she nodded. "*Oui.*"

"Great. Not far now," he sat back, looking pleased. "I heard from Angie this morning. She was excited to know I'll be buyin' the house. Turns out she's between jobs and would love to come spend some time with me. We'll get reacquainted. You know what I mean?" He regarded Elyse with an eager look on his face.

"*Je comprends*," she flicked a smile at him. "I understand."

She couldn't marry him, but should she still lend him the money? How could she let this man down so drastically when he was counting on her financial support? And why had she promised it in the first place? She groaned inwardly. What would her sons advise her to do? She'd been keeping quiet about the developing relationship between herself and Eddie. Very quiet. No one even suspected, or would suspect, that after only a few days she would have thought herself to care for the man. Not even her.

After all, she was no teenager, and should not be acting like one. Julien and Raphaël would counsel her to take more time before making such a huge decision, she knew it. Eddie would have to be told the bad news. She had been rash with her words and would now have to let him down as gently as possible.

They were through the village and heading along the road toward the turnout where she'd taken them for the hike. Elyse wasn't looking forward to it. She glanced at Eddie's profile. His jaw was set, and he leaned forward to scan the road ahead.

"Why don't you pull over there?" he pointed. It was on the opposite side of the road to where they'd parked before; a narrow, grassy trail leading into the trees. She shrugged. Certainly, there were fewer large stones to watch for, and the car didn't have much clearance after all.

Signalling, Elyse pulled onto the track, and they bumped along for a minute or two until it opened into a wider area where she could comfortably park the car. Eddie scrambled out and opened the back door, reaching for something.

"You brought water? And snacks?" she asked, stepping out to retrieve her hat and cross body bag from the back seat. She eyed the old rucksack of Julien's that Eddie pulled forth. It looked heavy. She settled her bag at her side and pushed back stray wisps of hair that had found their way over her eyes before pulling the hat onto her head. The early afternoon sun was boiling hot already.

"Yeah," he said, flinging it over his shoulders. "I asked your son if he had something I could use." Eddie slipped his thumbs under the straps on either side. He looked at her expectantly, as though last night had never happened. "Ready?"

She nodded and they marched back to the road, crossed over, and plunged into the *forêt de cèdres*.

It was a welcome relief to duck into the shade of the

forest. As the path was confined to a thin trail bordered by scrub brush, there was only room for them to walk single file. Eddie took the lead. Their footsteps were muffled on the carpet of pine needles and areas of bare ground. All that could be heard was the occasional rustle of a small animal in the underbrush, or birds fluttering in the branches high above.

How peaceful it all was. Elyse began to unwind, despite what was ahead.

Eddie led the way with long strides. She wondered for a moment why he seemed to be rushing, but then realized they had two events planned for today and this one had been his idea. He probably didn't want to hold them up for too long.

They resumed their former brooding silence as they trudged along the path, each lost in their own thoughts. At length, they came to the little stone bridge.

"Let's sit for a while. Okay?" Eddie asked.

In answer, she removed her sunglasses and lowered herself to the grassy rocks. This was it then, the moment of truth.

But instead of sitting, Eddie knelt in front of her, taking off the hat she'd bought him and smoothing his hair before capturing her hands in his.

Oh no. This was going to be worse than she'd thought.

"Elyse, I've said many times that I've fallen in love with you," he began in a low, hesitant voice. "And I want to give you one last chance to say you'll marry me." He played with her fingers and looked at the ground, appearing unsure of himself.

All Elyse was thinking about was the strange phrase, 'one last chance.' What kind of proposal was that? A chill ran down her spine despite the heat of the day.

"I'd cherish you," Eddie exclaimed and kept going on. His gaze flicked over her and then fixed on a spot over her head. "We could run your estate together or move to the house you're helping me buy. It would be up to you. What do you say? Will you marry me and make me the happiest man on earth?" He lowered his gaze and looked her in the eye. A nerve twitched in his temple, and he dragged a hand across his forehead to catch perspiration gathered there.

She took a long moment to respond. Had she not been plain enough last night, or had he just chosen not to listen?

"Eddie," she said gently. "We jumped into this too quickly. I really like you, but I can't even think about marriage at th—"

"You *like* me!" he sneered, dropping her hands as if they'd scalded him. He lunged backward through the leaves and dirt that had accumulated on the bridge for hundreds of years. "So, it's true. You don't love me. Is it because of Almond?" He scrambled up, his feet spaced wide apart with hands on hips as he bristled with sudden anger.

"This has nothing to do with Armand." Elyse moved to rise, but Eddie sprang forward and roughly pushed her down. Elyse felt a ball of fear form in her stomach. She licked her lips and tried again, saying whatever she thought might appease him. "Eddie," she forced a smile. "We haven't dated long enough. We need more—"

"But you love him and not me," he cut in again. "Is that it?" Eddie began to pace, running both hands through his hair. "I should have seen this coming. Why was I so blind?" He wheeled about and pointed an accusing finger.

"Why did you tease me?" he demanded. "You led me on to believe we had a future together. You made promises to me and I to you. Doesn't that mean anything?"

Elyse was alarmed. She glanced past Eddie, willing a

hiker to appear through the trees, but they were completely alone.

"Eddie," she said as steadily as she could, "I need you to stop and sit down. Just listen to what I was going to say without becoming upset."

"But I *am* upset," he ranted, increasing his pacing until he was walking in circles. "It's the same thing all over again. First Dad left and Mom died and then Kathy left me all alone. And now you. It's not my fault, I tell you," he cried, came to an abrupt halt in front of her, slamming a fist into the palm of his hand. He took a deep shuddering breath.

"I didn't want it to come to this," he cried. "I tried to give you another chance. You probably won't help me with the money either. Will you, dearest?"

Elyse thought hard, fear of inciting any further wrath flooded her body. She needed to keep her wits about her and try to remain calm. The man was unbalanced, or perhaps worse. She spoke in a placating tone, hoping to reason with him.

"I didn't say that, Eddie. All I said was that I couldn't marry you right now."

"Right *now*? Don't you mean *ever*?" he spat. "So, you'll give me the money?" he demanded, changing course abruptly. "Now?"

"What do you want? A certified check? 'Ard cash? Do you think I brought such things with me today?" She grabbed her purse and shook it. "Don't be ridiculous!" Elyse was getting angry. Who did this man think he was to demand such things of her? He was *not* the person she'd thought he was. He turned away groaning, his head bent. Somehow, she struggled to her feet. "I'm going 'ome."

Eddie roared with rage, whipping around and shoving her across the bridge. "Yes, as a matter of fact I want that money and a helluva lot more. You're not going anywhere until I get it," he snarled.

Elyse spun in a circle and fell, skidding on all fours across the stone bridge. She ground to a halt, having scraped both knees and the palms of her hands when she'd tried to break her fall. Shaken and scared, she flopped over to sit in the dirt, picking embedded pebbles and twigs from her hands. Her breathing came in great ragged gulps. She looked up at Eddie, refusing to give in to this madman. Slowly, she picked herself up.

"You will get nothing from me," she said loudly. His eyes narrowed dangerously. Coiled like a panther on the other side of the bridge, he waited for her next move. Shakily, she considered her options. Why had she worn a dress? She needed track shoes and jogging pants. But no. Here she was in a pretty dress and sandals. A trickle of blood ran down one leg. Her only hope would be to forget the path and dash down into the undergrowth, splash across the stream, and make a run for it. After all, she had the keys.

Her glance betrayed her. With a cruel smile Eddie charged at her, pinning her arms behind her back until she yelped with pain.

"Guess what? I don't need you to get me nothin'," he growled into her ear. "That lovin' family of yours will pay to get you back. And I know just where to keep you until they do." Eddie dropped her arms and grabbed a fistful of her dress. Using one leg, he whipped her feet out from under her then lowered her to the ground, ramming her face into the dirt. He placed his knee on the small of her back, holding her in place.

Elyse struggled, trying in vain to twist herself from his grasp, to roll, kick, or claw any part of him she could reach.

But he held her securely. Producing a length of rope from the sack, he bound her hands tightly.

Then, he pulled her upright until she was only centimetres away from his sneering face. She glared at him. "I had you figured, didn't I?' he ground out between clenched teeth. "You weren't gonna give me the money I asked for, were ya? Well, now I want more. Two million euros should set me up nicely."

Elyse itched to knock that cocky grin off his face, but her wrists already burned from struggling against the rope. Instead, she lifted her foot and kicked him as hard as she could. Her foot hit him on the shin. She'd have aimed a little higher, but they stood too close for her to achieve it.

Yowling in pain, Eddie took a step back, reaching instinctively for his leg and releasing her. Elyse toppled sideways, caught herself and dashed down to the creek bed where she fell in a tangled heap on the slippery rocks. She was sobbing by the time his shoes appeared in her blurred vision. How would she ever escape this crazed lunatic?

Eddie hauled her up and stood her in front of him again. Icy water from the mountain brook gurgled over their feet. "You're forgettin' somethin'." His face got closer and more menacing. He showered her with droplets of saliva as he threw venomous words into her face. "Your family don't know nothin' about this. They don't really know me, my name, where I'm from, nothin'. But I know where they live, and they trust me. Especially that sweet little granddaughter of yours. So, you'd better do what I say, or I'll go back there and make them sorry they ever laid eyes on me."

Terror clawed at Elyse's chest. Celeste? Was he that much of a monster? But she couldn't be sure of anything anymore. Obediently she allowed herself to be dragged back to the path and when he prodded her, indicating she walk farther into the forest, she did so without question.

Elyse stumbled along the trail. Her head hurt and her eyesight was blurry from tears and dirt. The strap of one sandal had broken and kept tripping her. She paused a second to kick it to the side of the little-used path. For a moment she felt a ray of hope. Perhaps her shoe might be a clue that she had passed this way. But no one knew where they'd been going. And even if they did, there were hundreds of trails in the forest.

Armand. She pictured him in her mind's eye, tall and handsome, laughing with her over some silly joke as he pruned the rose bushes. Or him smiling as they tended the rosemary in the herb garden before plucking a few sprigs for the roast pork they would have that evening. She remembered how they had traversed this very path; enjoying one another's company, compatible and happy.

Her mind flitted to that fateful morning when he had tried, ever so gently, to express his feelings for her. His true feelings, she thought bitterly. Not trumped-up ones in order to deceive and take advantage of her kindness. She'd been foolish and weak. Falling for the smooth speech of a man she didn't know, and now she and her family would pay for her mistake.

How could she have been so stupid? Head hanging, she berated herself over and over, worrying that she had unalterably hurt the man who truly loved her.

After what felt like an eternity, Elyse stepped onto gravel, the sharp stones hurting her bare foot. She jolted to a halt so suddenly that Eddie bumped into her from behind. He pushed her forward with an expletive. She saw where they were going—to the abandoned house, of course.

He left her to carefully pick her way through the stones

along the neglected old driveway and went ahead to wrestle with the gate. Again, he swung the pack from his back and withdrew a pair of wire cutters which he used to make short work of the lock that barred entry to the home.

"Go through!" he barked, throwing the gate wide. Elyse hobbled into the front yard, stepping along the overgrown sidewalk on her way to the front steps. No one had been here for more than fifty years. She cast a fleeting glance to the rows of dirty windows on the third and fourth floors. They were like sightless, brooding eyes. Maybe this place was haunted with ghosts, as Armand had told her was the local superstition.

Eddie pushed past her, bounded up the front steps, and stood on the rickety veranda looking both ways as though to ensure they were alone. But of course, they were alone, Elyse thought furiously. No one ever came here. The lack of a road spoke volumes. She would never be found.

The porch floorboards creaked under his weight as he moved to the door and rattled the handle. Naturally, it was locked. Undeterred, Eddie walked to one of the many windows that, remarkably had remained unbroken. Until today.

Turning his face away and rolling down his shirt sleeve, Eddie smashed it in with his elbow. Shards of glass flew everywhere.

"Stay there or I'll catch you and make you sorry!" he threatened.

She was already sorry. How could it get any worse?

Eddie bashed away the remaining glass, threw one leg over the sill, clutched the top with both hands, and swung inside. In moments he had opened the front door and beckoned to her with a scowl. She hesitated briefly, then plodded in. He slammed the door, and she heard him lock it behind them. She gave one despairing glance out the nearest window as he propelled her toward a door leading to another room, but she could barely see through the grimy pane of glass. The once white lace curtains hung in shreds. Yet it obscured the outside world quite effectively. She was well and truly hidden now.

The room had been grand at one time. Paint and tattered, rose-covered wallpaper peeled from the walls in huge strips, and a dusty, but ornate chandelier hung precariously at an odd angle. Spider webs festooned the rest of the ceiling and dipped down to adorn the faces of long-since-dead men and women who stared grimly from their portraits. Fifties era furniture, covered in patterned shades of faded gold, hunched amongst an assortment of crates and boxes. They had been hastily filled with items like ornaments and dishes, and then left to rot across a fraying carpet.

Except Eddie was not satisfied with this room. She suspected he didn't want her anywhere close to the front of the house on the off chance someone might come by or be looking for her. She didn't see how that might ever happen.

They entered a long hallway with closed doors leading off at intervals. Again, he shoved her. It wasn't necessary, since she was moving. Although she was slow and limped from the loss of her sandal and the tenderness of her bare foot. He seemed to delight in asserting his power over her. Elyse stumbled. She felt weak and ached all over, but regained her balance before she fell. She wouldn't give him the satisfaction of tumbling at his feet. She swallowed tears of pain and fear, took a deep breath, and plodded on.

Finally, they came to the last door at the very end of the hall. Eddie knocked her aside as he moved past her to open it and look inside. Looking beyond him, she saw it was the kitchen. Black and, what must have been white checker-board tiles covered the floor and the wall to their left was almost completely adorned with brass pots and pans, their shiny exteriors tarnished. The opposite wall housed cupboards, generous countertops, a massive refrigerator with the door hanging by one hinge, and a huge black stove on which to cook meals for Hollywood's elite. Straight ahead, windows ran almost the entire length of the room, surprisingly still intact despite the thick branches that pushed against the glass from the outside. It was a jungle out there. Elyse longed to escape into the tangle of those trees and flee this madness.

Reaching back, Eddie yanked Elyse through the door and shut it with an ominous click.

"Welcome to your new home dearest," he said nastily. "Not quite as grand as the last one, but close, don't you think?"

A long table ran down the middle of the rectangular space with a few rickety wooden chairs. He shoved her down onto one and used the rope around her wrists to secure her to the rungs at her back.

"Now, your purse," he said, pawing for the bag that dangled at her side. He snapped the strap in one motion and held it in front of her nose. "You have a couple of texts to send, and I believe the phone numbers I need. Besides, you won't be using it again. Or these." He jangled her keys from the end of his pinky and laughed.

Eddie flicked on her phone, scrolled down to what he wanted and entered the numbers into his own flip phone. Then, he typed a couple of texts on hers and took a picture of her, bedraggled and strapped to a chair. He jabbed at the buttons, sending ransom notes, she assumed, to her family.

"That should get a little action out of those sons of

yours," he said. "If they ever want to see you alive again, that is." He chuckled.

Elyse thought of movies she'd watched where the police were able to trace the location of a cellular phone. Maybe…

Almost as if he could read her mind, he spoke once more. "I wouldn't be that stupid, Elyse," he said, powering off her device. He dropped it to the flagstones and stomped on it until the phone was in pieces. "You think this is my first rodeo?" he barked. "At least part of what I told you was true. I lost my daughter, not because I was out of town for work. No—I got caught, but only once, and spent some time in jail. But I wised up and that'll never happen again." He shot her an evil smile as her eyes widened.

"*C'est vrai. Tu n'es pas mon premier, et tu ne seras pas mon dernier.*" Eddie spoke in perfect French, assuring her it was true. She was not his first scam and certainly if he had his way, would not be his last.

She swallowed; her throat parched. "Who are you? Where are you really from?" she asked in French, realizing he understood every word. "You don't work importing olive oil, do you?"

He laughed. The sound was hollow and ominous in the deserted kitchen.

"What do *you* think?" he said with a mocking arch of his eyebrows. "I'm not about to give you any details. But I've lived in France for about twenty years now, doing what I do best." He ended this statement with an up-tilt of his chin, as though he was proud of his accomplishments in the world of fraud, deception, and burglary. He tossed his glasses onto the table. "I'm sick of wearin' these."

"You are despicable." Elyse could not even stand to look at the man. She averted her eyes to the tangled masses of fruit trees that grew just outside the back door and were curled against the windows. She was furious with him, but more with herself for being so easily duped.

"Maybe," he agreed, "but I think we can both agree that I'm the one in control of this situation, so by default, I win." He chuckled and lifted her chin with a finger. "Sorry, my dear, but I have business to attend to. I trust you'll be okay on your own. Maybe there's a few rats in this place. I'll bet they'd like a friend. Or snakes. You Frogs got any poisonous snakes around here that might hole up in an old abandoned house?" He laughed cruelly. "Oh yeah, and did you want a kiss before I leave, dearest? No? Well, how about another length of rope to keep you nice and safe until I return?"

He pulled more cord from the bag and snapped it between his hands. Then, despite her futile attempts to kick him away, he lashed her feet to the chair and stood, dusting off his hands. "Don't go running off now," he said. After sliding his phone into a pocket and shrugging on the backpack, he turned to leave.

"You can't leave me here!" shrieked Elyse, a sudden fear consuming her. But he was already gone.

What if he never returned? What if she slowly died, strapped to a chair, in an abandoned mansion in the countryside? She would never see her loved ones again. Even her corpse would not be found. And her family would frantically search, never knowing what had happened.

Panic rose like bile in the back of her throat. She choked. Spluttering and sobbing her fear into the overwhelming silence, she wailed for help. But the house did not care. Silent and foreboding, the walls closed in around her as the sunlight drained from the sky.

Chapter Thirteen

Elyse's eyes shot open as a door banged, reverberating through the house. Then footsteps and eventually a light crept through the cracks around the kitchen door where she was imprisoned. She tensed. Screwing her eyes shut she prayed fervently that it would not be Eddie. Anyone but him, she begged, but when the door slammed open, bashing into the wall next to her, it was Eddie's shadowy face that greeted her. Her heart clenched.

"*Est-ce que je t'ai manqué?*" He mocked her, asking if she had missed him as she might have done yesterday morning, or the day before when she'd been fool enough to believe he cared for her. He threw a sleeping bag and pillow on the filthy floor and walked in front of her chair to train the beam of a long flashlight into her face.

Tilting his head to one side, he regarded her disdainfully. "What? You didn't miss me—dearest love?" He threw back his head and laughed, gripping her chin with punishing fingers and squeezing till Elyse thought her bones would break. Her eyes watered from the pain, but she refused to give him the satisfaction of crying out. His hand felt hot and sticky. She cringed and struggled to escape from his grasp. How could she have ever thought herself to care for this horrible excuse for a man?

He shoved her away from him and the chair teetered precariously. "You seemed to like my kisses pretty well yesterday," he spat, bringing his face close. "I wonder how Almond would feel about that?"

Elyse shrank back, refusing to answer his taunting questions. She'd been so foolish. Drawing in a ragged breath, she tried to gather her thoughts. Could she ask if he'd contacted her sons? She needed to ask if they were coming for her, but knew only too well that they weren't. They had no idea where she was. In the end, she didn't have to ask. Eddie was so pleased with himself and wanting to show off that he filled her in on his recent activities.

He rocked on his heels and crossed his arms, much like a preening rooster. "I made the call from a blocked phone number and set the ransom at two million, just like I said." Eddie glowed eerily in the light of his flashlight. He set the tiny, battery-powered lamp on the nearby table and rubbed his hands together with glee. "Now we wait till morning." He looked at his watch as though somehow it would make the time go faster.

Triumphantly, he grinned. "If the bank opens at nine and I get the money transferred to my account before noon, which is what I told them must happen if they ever wanted to see you alive again, I'll tell them where they can find you...then our little transaction will be only a memory," he said. "Oh, but don't make the mistake of thinking I can be traced. I have ways of disappearing that even Houdini would be envious of."

Elyse stared at his fiendish face in the glowing lamplight.

She had no idea who Houdini was, and didn't care, but she worried about her family and the torment they must be going through right now. She studied the man before her. How could someone be so cleverly deceptive as this? Evil and conniving. She twisted in her seat, trying to relieve the growing pain in her wrists and shoulders from having her hands bound behind her for so long.

"I'm thirsty," she said, licking her dry lips. "And I assume you have water and food for yourself. Could you untie me for a moment and let me have a sip?" She had to go to the bathroom too, but didn't think he'd let her outside by herself. She refused to be watched by the likes of this monster.

He looked at her suspiciously. "I'm not untying you. I don't care if your arms fall off. I'll hold a bottle of water to your mouth." His teeth flashed white in the beam as he grinned. "It's kind of romantic, don't you think?"

Elyse gritted her teeth. If she wasn't so thirsty, she'd have told him where he could put his water bottle, but she needed a drink badly. Her throat was parched.

Unscrewing a bottle, he moved toward her. His thumb gently grazed her dry lips before he swung his hand back and slapped her face. Her head rocketed back; her cheek hot and burning. Her face throbbed with unexpected pain and she licked her lips, tasting blood.

Eddie chuckled. Placing one hand on the back of her neck he wound his fingers into her hair and forced her head back, while the other hand held the water to her lips. As she opened her mouth, he jammed it against her teeth, and tipped the bottle fully upright. The water coursed into her mouth, down her chin and over her neck and chest. She gulped noisily, feeling like she was drowning. Her eyes flicked up in mute appeal. Still, he held her in place, pouring the water down her throat until she gagged and almost vomited.

Eddie was laughing again, toying with her to see how she might react to the threat of her own demise. Finally, he relented. He flipped her upright and she bowed her head, coughing and spluttering. Elyse struggled to catch her breath, her chest heaving with the effort. She glared at his smug face, but he only smiled in return. Hatred flooded her heart.

"Still love me dearest?" he asked, bending to peer at her. "What a shame," he clicked his tongue sadly. "Your pretty dress got wet. Did you wear it just for me?" He flicked the collar.

Elyse closed her eyes and fought to bring her anger and frustration under control. Giving in to her emotions and panic wouldn't help. She had to think of a way out of this. Perhaps it was only a dream. Things like this only happened to beautiful young women in late night movies. Not to aging widows who lived quiet lives tending gardens and playing with their grandchildren. Surely not. If she could have pinched herself, just to be sure, she would have.

Elyse began to shiver uncontrollably. Shock was setting in along with the coolness of the night. Every part of her body ached from the violence of her shudders, but she couldn't stop. Eddie ignored her, even though the sound of her chattering teeth filled the empty space. In a corner, not far from her, he prepared his sleeping arrangements. Then, with a yawn, he climbed beneath a blanket, pulling the warmth over his shoulders and arranging a camp pillow to his liking.

"Sweet dreams dearest," he murmured sarcastically, as he had said to her the night before. Extinguishing the light, he rolled onto his side and minutes later she heard his gentle snores. He had fallen asleep with a clear conscience, she supposed. She, on the other hand, sat upright and vibrating, her mind and body suffering physical as well as mental anguish.

If only she had handled things differently, none of this would have happened. Was she worth two million euros? Not at this point. She felt useless—and like a fool. A woman who was too old to be in this predicament, and so trusting of a wolf in sheep's clothing. This whole situation proved she didn't deserve Armand's love anyway. Especially not now, even though her heart ached at the thought of never seeing him again. He was a good man, dependable, trustworthy, and the best friend she'd ever had. Too bad she'd destroyed their relationship for the sake of false emotions. Was she even aware of what her true feelings were? Clearly, she was unable to rightly judge between fact and fiction or whether someone was unhinged. The evidence was snoring across the room.

If she got back home alive, she would be content with a solitary life. She would be glad to exist only for the benefit of her family. If they were forced to pay so much for her release, though, she doubted she would ever get over the shame of it.

As these thoughts chased one another through her brain, her body calmed. Tremors came in spurts and then subsided. Despite the complete darkness that surrounded her, Elyse opened her eyes and looked toward the windows for the friendly silver moon. She knew it must be nearing fullness. It had been close two nights ago when she and Eddie had shared a meal in Lacoste.

What desecration! Fiercely she berated herself for taking him to the same spot she had shared with her precious

Armand. She squinted into the darkness, willing some glimmer of light to appear. And then it did.

The merest hint of a silvery glow touched the branches of the trees outside. As she watched, the light grew, bathing the world outside this creaky old house in an ethereal luminosity.

Her eyes filled with tears. Not tears from fear, or pain, or frustration at her captivity, but tears that spilled from her eyes at the beauty of creation, the endless hope of renewal, and the mystical, silvery moon that heralded it.

And then a shadowy something moved. It was large, and creeping from beyond the tangle of bushes outside this deserted old house. Elyse sucked in a breath and held it, watching. What was it? An animal? A ghost? Blood pumped through her veins, and she felt her every heartbeat. Afraid to blink, lest she miss seeing whatever it was again, she stared, wide-eyed into the moonlit garden of a bygone era.

There it was again! It was a person; she was sure of it— a man. But what sort of person would be lurking outside this derelict building in the dead of night? A flash of light sped across the window. They had a flashlight. Who would be poking around outside? They couldn't be up to any good. What fresh horror was in store for her? She slumped down, pulling at her bonds as though magically they would come undone, allowing her to escape this nightmare. However, her efforts were fruitless.

Muted sounds of a body scraping past twigs and branches filtered through the timeworn kitchen walls. Suddenly the silhouette of a face loomed at the window.

Elyse screamed. In a move purely instinctive, she thrust herself backward in the chair and toppled with a crunch onto her back.

"What's going on?" Eddie shouted. He clambered to his

feet and flicked on the flashlight to beam it around the room. It came to rest on Elyse who was squirming on the floor. "What are you doing?" he hollered, rushing over to aim a kick at her. "That scared me half to death."

"A rat…I—I saw a rat."

Elyse fell silent as he accepted her explanation with a grunt. She found, to her delight, that the ancient wooden chair had broken. Her hands and feet were still tied—but no longer were they bound to the chair. As Eddie moved about the room, checking for why she had screamed, she stretched out. She revelled in the small amount of newfound freedom, then lay still, not wishing to draw attention to the fact. In wiggling her hands, however, she found that, minus two rungs of the chair, the rope had loosened. With concentrated effort, she pulled her right hand free, and the rope dropped off her left. She began to work on her ankles, but the knots were rock solid.

Eddie snatched another of the seats and, breathing heavily, made to sit down, but a noise from outside distracted him. He swivelled to flash his light across the windows, but there was nothing. With long strides he approached them, leaning across the crumbling countertops and holding the light up high so he could look outside.

And at that moment the back door crashed to the floor, splitting into a thousand shards of splintered wood.

Armand tumbled in with it.

For a moment he swayed, off balance with the effort it had taken to bash down the door, but righted himself immediately. He crouched on top of the shattered door like a coiled spring, then hurled himself across the room to where Eddie was frozen in amazement. A shout of fury erupted from Armand's chest as he attacked the man.

Elyse's heart almost burst. *Armand, had come for her!* She

scrabbled across the floor with her hands and her still-tied feet, worked herself up against the wall and pushed her body into a seated position.

Armand threw the first punch, catching Eddie across the jaw. He reeled back, falling into the wall of copper pans. With a deafening crash they clattered to the floor along with the man.

Armand followed him down He snatched Eddie by the collar and heaved him upright with one hand while he lifted his fist to deliver another bone-cracking punch with the other. But Eddie flung himself to one side, evading Armand. He broke free. Eddie fell to his knees but scrambled up immediately. The torch flew through the air, skittering to a stop several metres from Elyse. The light flickered and went out. The room plunged into darkness.

"So, you came to find your girlfriend," Eddie's rasping voice split the air. "Isn't that just sickeningly sweet. You might like to know I learned karate in high school. You don't have a chance against me. Why not give up now and I'll let you both live?"

Shuffling movements told Elyse he was edging toward her. She couldn't let that happen though. Eddie wouldn't use her as a pawn a second time. The torch was close. She knew roughly where it was, despite the inky darkness of the room. Cautiously, she slid down, flattened herself, and rolled.

"I'm not afraid of you," Armand's deep voice flooded Elyse's senses. Love and gratitude filled her being. She had thought she might never hear him speak again. Eddie stopped. Elyse paused a fraction of a second until further shuffling noises covered her movements, then she rolled again.

"And here's something *you* don't know…" Armand said in a quiet, conversational tone. "I would *die* to save her."

The world ground to a shuddering halt.

Elyse lay on the filthy floor staring at a shaft of moonlight on the ceiling. Had he really just said that? Her chest heaved as sobs begged for release. Armand loved her. Even after all this—he loved her. She longed to speak, to scream that she loved him too, but she couldn't. Not now. Not when such a menace lurked in the shadows beside her. She swallowed it down and rolled.

"You're more of a fool than I thought," came Eddie's furious response.

Once more, her eyes adjusted to the shimmering glow of moonlight. Even though the two broad kitchen windows were dirty, enough of the moon's light filtered through that she saw the two men's shapes. Armand was in pursuit. Metal pans clanged together as he waded through the debris. But Eddie was coming after her. She knew it. She had to keep searching for the light and moving away from the madman.

Elyse bonked into something. The table. Reaching out, she followed the leg up until she reached the corner, then she ran a hand along the underside of the sturdy piece of furniture. It would help with safety if she could stay under it. Pulling herself onto her knees, she continued her search across the floor, frantically looking for the lost light as she dragged herself along. If she could just shine it on Eddie, she felt sure Armand would win any contest of strength. He wasn't just a chef, chopping leafy greens and crushing garlic all day. She knew for a fact he belonged to a boxing club in the city, and he was strong.

"Where are you, Elyse?" Eddie whispered in a sing-song

falsetto. His hands grasped the wood over her head. She lurched back, banging into the torch. It rolled away.

"Ah, there you are dearest." Eddie's voice came closer as his hand swiped through the air. He caught the material of her dress and fisted it. Then he backed up, dragging her with him. Elyse just had time to wrap her fingers around the metal cylinder of the flashlight and bring it along.

But Eddie hadn't reckoned on her hands being free. Or on her will to fight back. At the same moment as she flicked on the light, Elyse brought it down with all her strength on his arms. He yelped and let go, his scowling face coming into sharp relief.

Now it was his turn to be dragged. Quick as lightning, Armand was behind him. He wrapped an arm around Eddie's neck and yanked him away from her. She maintained her position, holding the light on the two men. Without warning, Eddie threw himself forward and Armand flew over his head. He landed flat on his back in the rubble of the destroyed door.

Eddie was on him in a flash. They thrashed back and forth across the room, grunting and groaning with effort. Powerful arms swung, and legs churned in the spotlight of Elyse's beam. First one got the upper hand, then the other.

Swooping down, Eddie snatched up a heavy, cast-iron frying pan and with both hands he swung it. Armand lifted an arm to protect himself, but the pan smacked him across the side of his head with deadly accuracy.

Clang! The blow reverberated throughout the room and Eddie whooped with satisfaction as Armand dropped to his knees. Elyse screamed as Armand toppled over like dead weight. Somehow, she scuttled across the floor to him, tears flowing down her face. She kept the light fixed on him, praying he was still alive.

But Armand surprised them both. As Eddie turned away with a victorious cry, Armand kicked out one leg and caught Elyse's captor behind the knees. Eddie crumpled. As he went down, Armand slowly rose. He threw back his arm and slammed Eddie with a right hook that would have felled a tree.

Eddie dropped to the floor, unconscious.

Armand sank onto the tiles and would have hit hard too if Elyse had not broken his fall. She cradled this brave, wonderful man in her arms, rocking him back and forth as endearments tumbled from her lips. She kissed his forehead and stroked his hair, smoothed the lines on his face and dropped more kisses, along with tears onto his cheeks.

And when he opened his eyes and looked at her, great wracking sobs finally broke free from her body.

Armand raised a hand to her face, cupping her cheek and giving her a wobbly smile.

"*Je t'aime, tu sais*," he whispered.

"I love you too. So very much. I am so sorry for not knowing it from the start."

"Shh…No apologies." Armand came up on one elbow, wincing as he felt the growing lump on his head. In the dim light, he looked at Eddie sprawled across the floor. "I think we had better make use of your rope, my love, and then I will call the authorities."

First, Armand released the knot around her ankles and then, guided by the torch, he secured the ropes in the same manner around Eddie's wrists and ankles. The man didn't even stir as they worked. Only then, Armand called the police. He handed the phone to her so she could call her family and let them know she was safe.

Julien reacted with a shout and loud praise for Armand. Elyse heard Raphaël whoop as he roared his love and thanks into the phone too. Angelina was in the background, calming baby Celeste when all the yelling scared her. Even Lia, Elyse's daughter, was at the chateau. Elyse heard her demand to speak to their mother.

"Mom," she sobbed into the phone. "I can't believe this happened to you, but I'm so grateful you're okay. I'm staying right here until you get home, so I can wrap my arms around you. I love you. And Armand!"

More tears rolled down Elyse's cheeks. She was so blessed to have her family and, as Lia had pointed out, Armand.

In between the emergency call, and the time it took for the authorities to arrive, Armand explained how he had found her and why he had come alone. They sat on the floor, their backs against the wall, hands clasped. Elyse still found it hard to wrap her head around what had just happened.

With his eyes shut against the pain in his head, Armand began. "I was at the chateau for much of the afternoon, in order to plan the party, so I heard the pandemonium that ensued after Eddie sent the texts demanding money for your release," he said, launching into the tale. "Of course, Julien called a family meeting immediately and we were all included. Thankfully, Aunt Marie was there also. She was the only one who had a clue as to your whereabouts. We were frantic with worry," he concluded, holding a palm to his forehead and squeezing her hand with the other.

"Yes, Marie was there when Eddie asked me to take him for a walk in the cedar forest," Elyse said, remembering. "Thank goodness!"

"It helped. We had no idea where to start until then. But even with that knowledge, it only narrowed the search area by a small margin, since the forests of the Luberon are huge. That was, until I'd gone back to my apartment and thought about it. I recalled how much you had enjoyed the particular trail we'd taken last year. And how you were enthralled with the story of this chateau and the movie actress who died, leaving it to her argumentative offspring."

"That's why you came alone?"

He went to nod, but then clutched his head and groaned. "Yes," he said. "It was already ten o'clock at night. I didn't want to disturb anyone, even though your sons were likely still awake and pacing the floor. It was a hunch and I acted on it immediately."

"You came for me," Elyse sighed with happiness. She didn't deserve this man, but she was so very grateful. Then a thought crossed her mind. It was a long shot, but she had to ask it anyhow. "Did you walk up the path and find my shoe?"

Armand's lips formed a crooked smile, and he reached behind his back to pull forth her sandal. The broken strap dangled in the fitful light. He shrugged. "I knew it was yours and I kept it. I'll always come when you need me, Elyse. You are my Cinderella after all," he said softly.

"And you," she said, leaning in to tenderly kiss his lips, "are my Prince Charming."

Epilogue

Elyse would not allow the party to be cancelled. It went ahead regardless of what she had been through the day before. After the police had come and taken Eddie away, shouting and swearing, Armand and Elyse had driven to the police station and their statements had been taken.

It turned out that Eddie had indeed been in France, evading the authorities for the past twenty years. That was about the only thing he hadn't lied about. His real name was Samuel Reed. He'd been involved in petty theft all of his life and had been jailed for extortion and kidnapping almost thirty years ago. The officer who took her statement, told Elyse that no one understood how he'd managed to get to France. However, they imagined it was the work of a friend employed by the passport services in the States that had got him here. Then, he'd spread his web of deceit and lies, primarily conning women into giving him money by offering wealthy widows promises of marriage and true love. Sadly, some of them had not survived their encounter with the monster. He was convincing and handsome, Elyse knew. She felt sorry for the other women he'd destroyed.

The import company Eddie had said he worked for didn't exist either. All documents he'd given to Julien the previous year had been falsified in order to set up his plan to seduce Elyse this summer. Elyse knew he hadn't intended to marry her. He was a classic con artist.

After that, she and Armand had gone to the hospital to be checked. He did indeed have a concussion, but insisted he would take it easy for a few days and do his best to avoid further fistfights with convicted felons, at least for a couple of weeks.

She smiled at her mirror, thinking how he had retained his sense of humour, even after what had happened. Thankfully, all of that was behind her. It was so good to be home. She smoothed a stray lock of hair and surveyed her reflection. She'd purposely chosen a ruby-red, full-skirted dress today, knowing it was Armand's favourite colour. It suited her glossy, chestnut hair and fell in flattering folds, hiding her sore and bandaged knees. Her body and face were bruised and scratched, but she felt lucky to be alive. It could have easily been the end for her.

She secured the matching belt around her small waist to accentuate her figure. Sure, maybe her curves were a little more generous than they had been when she was twenty-five, but she was happy with the overall result.

She strung a milky-white string of pearls around her neck and added matching earrings. They had been her mother's and she wanted as many reminders of those she loved around her today, as possible. Lastly, she searched for sandals. She picked up the damaged one that Armand had found along the cedar path and stared at it for a moment before setting it on her dresser. It had gotten lost during the fight with Eddie, but Armand had insisted on hunting for the flimsy shoe until it was found. It had helped to lead him to her, he'd said, and deserved to be restored. So, she had brought it home. Not as a memento of the horrible mistakes she'd made with Eddie, but of the love she had found with Armand.

Tears pricked her eyes, and she pulled a tissue from a box on her bureau and dabbed them. Then she pulled two more and stuffed them into a hidden pocket of her dress, foreseeing she would be needing them today.

She hurried downstairs to find Marie busy in the kitchen along with Clarisse, the young girl who came to clean the house, and two young men who had been hired for the occasion. She had insisted that Armand not have anything to do with the work today. He was her guest and she smiled at the term. He wasn't that either, but she had yet to classify him as her boyfriend. It felt too juvenile of a word to use for what they shared.

Slipping into the kitchen unobtrusively, she made herself a coffee and snatched a croissant, a napkin, some jam, and a knife before retiring to the patio. It was peaceful. This afternoon friends and family would come to celebrate the arrival of Celeste, the latest Belliveau child into their midst and Elyse could hardly wait. She glanced up as Lia joined her. Although she was the eldest child, Lia didn't look her age. She swished through the door in a floor-length, halter-neck style gown of jade-green, with beads and rhinestones glittering on the bodice in the morning sun.

Lia, her petite, dark-haired daughter set her drink on the table and stooped to hold her mother in her arms. She gently kissed Elyse on both cheeks four, no, five times.

Carefully, she leaned back in her chair laughing. Everything ached. "I'm so glad you stayed overnight, sweetheart," she said, picking up her knife and preparing to eat.

"I couldn't leave. Not after almost losing you to that monster." Lia pulled a chair close to her. "I haven't been spending enough time with you anyway," she raised a hand as Elyse began to protest. "I know what you're going to say. I have a family of my own and a job teaching school. It's true. But family is what matters." Her eyes brimmed as she gazed at her mother.

Elyse reached for her hand. "I am happy to have you with me whenever you can arrange to come," she said.

They sat together discussing the day's events and drinking their coffee until movement caught Elyse's eye. It was Armand.

Without another thought, she flew from her chair and went to him. He opened his arms wide and held her as tight as both their sore bodies would allow. "Don't ever let me go," she said in a muffled voice against his chest.

"I don't intend to," he said.

Pulling back, she looked anxiously into his face. "Are you alright? Your 'ead…" she reached out a hand and smoothed it over his brow. "My dear, sweet Armand."

He caught her hand and pressed it to his lips. "Knowing you are safe is all that matters to me. Bruises and a concussion will heal." He lowered her hand and looked earnestly into her eyes. "Could you go for a walk with me in the garden like we always used to do? Before this big day begins."

"Of course." She turned to tell her beloved daughter what they were doing only to find Lia had discreetly left them alone.

She grinned at him and shrugged, moving to thread her arm through his as they strolled along the well-worn path.

They continued into the garden away from the prying eyes of the people working in the kitchen.

"The herbs are doing well," he remarked, as they drew abreast of the rosemary bush and passed a bed of basil.

"*Oui*," said Elyse, her mind wandering.

"And the moonflowers appear to be blooming steadily."

"It's true."

"How are the begonias?" he asked, shooting her a serious look.

"I don't care about them," she answered.

"What?" he said, drawing to a stop beside their favourite bench and pulling her down to sit beside him.

"I said, I don't care about the begonias."

"Oh," he said mildly. "What *do* you care about?"

"You," she said in a small voice, before taking a deep breath of the aromatic air that wafted around them.

"I see." Armand slowly swivelled to face her and took both of her hands in his. He was so handsome today. He wore a black button-up shirt that fit his lean body like a glove and dark grey slacks, the cuffs turned up to expose a small amount of ankle above his stylish black loafers. Taking a deep breath, his eyes darkened as they dropped to her mouth. And then he kissed her, a long, lingering kiss that left her breathless.

"You 'ave no idea 'ow long I've wanted to do that," he murmured into her ear as he gathered her into his arms. As she opened her mouth to apologize, once again, he pressed a finger to her lips. "No," he said. "I would wait an eternity to spend time with you like this. But there is one thing I would like to ask you."

"*Oui*?" she said as he paused and gazed across the garden.

He looked back at her, searching her face as he cupped

her cheeks with gentle hands. "Elyse, you have been my friend, my confidant, my inspiration. I love you as I have loved no other. Will you—will you be my wife?" he proposed, but quickly added, "If you need more time to think, I will give you all the time that you need. But I promise to be here for you—now and forever."

Elyse needed nothing more. "And I promise to be here for you, Armand. I would love to be your wife."

She melted into his arms with a sigh and nestled against him.

And the Garden of Promises, wherein their destiny had grown, now bore witness to their love.

vinci-books.com/moonlightoverthecinqueterre

Love is sweeter the second time around.

Against the backdrop of Italy's stunning coastline, Sarah and Raphaël confront their past and fight for their future. Can they overcome suspicion and deceit to rekindle their long-lost love?

Turn the page for a free preview…

Moonlight Over the Cinque Terre: Chapter One

"I'm sorry Tyler. But no, I can't marry you." Sarah lowered her gaze from his hopeful eyes, to where he knelt in a flowerbed, crushing a patch of her mother's pink petunias. It was the worst possible time for him to ask her, as it was just before she was to leave the country. Awkward too, since she'd asked Tyler to walk with her in order to break off their relationship for good this time. She stared down at the oversized grey sweatpants she wore and shoved her hands into the matching hoodie, her long blonde hair falling across her face. She would let him down gently.

As she took a breath to explain herself, he snapped open the lid of a small, blue velvet box and caught her wrist, endeavoring to thrust the case into her hand. "Just look at it." His eyes entreated her. "I picked out a diamond you'll love. Of course, it's smaller than I'd like, but someday, when I take over your family business…" He coughed, his cheeks reddening. "Anyway, it will mean a lot to me if you'd wear it."

Sarah took a step back and snatched her hand away.

She could feel a headache brewing. Wait, Tyler planned on taking over her father's drilling company? When had that been discussed? He knew nothing about the oil business, always saying that working on the rigs her father owned was too dangerous.

Her parents liked her boyfriend, but for him to think he'd take over the company her father had spent his lifetime building, was presumptuous. Just like Tyler expecting she'd marry him after casually dating for a mere two months. She stared at him in shock.

"We don't have to set a date yet," he continued, jumping up to knock the dirt from his faded jeans. "Why don't you wear the ring as a promise? We can discuss dates...our future later when you get back from Italy."

"It's no good." Sarah protested. "I've told you several times I'm not ready for this. I won't agree to marry you or accept your ring." A sudden movement caused Sarah to glance toward the house where she caught sight of Jim. He was one of the gardeners who'd been with her parents since they bought the estate near Edmonton, Alberta. The man peered at them over a hedge he was trimming. Catching her eye, he ducked out of sight.

"How long do you need?" Tyler persisted, oblivious to all but his insistence that Sarah accept his proposal. "I love you, Sarah."

Sarah sighed. "Yes, you've been telling me that for a while now. But you won't consider the fact that I don't love you." She felt as though she were being harsh, but enough was enough. She didn't want to lead him on any longer and he wouldn't take no for an answer. "We've known one another almost two years now and dated for a few months, but even you have to admit we are more like friends than anything. We don't have what it takes to be married." She moved away from him and began walking toward the house. "You've got to stop this. Honestly Tyler, I don't think you love me as much as you imagine you do either," she muttered.

"I totally think we have what it takes," he stated irritably. "You just won't let me close enough to prove it." Disregarding her last statement, he increased his pace to stay abreast of her, shoving the ring box into the pocket of his jeans and irritably tucking in his white t-shirt.

She stole a sideways glance at him. Tyler was a good-looking man with a long, sandy-colored mop of hair that he kept out of his face with frequent flips of his head. He was tall, slim, and his shoulders were thrown back and erect as he strode beside her, his face looking like thunder. Usually his mischievous hazel eyes, a ready smile, and a quick wit made him fun to be with—but at the moment those attributes were replaced with a sullen frown.

Sarah stopped, exasperated. "How can you say that? The fact is, we don't have any chemistry and very little in common. We've been together almost every day and that hasn't changed."

"And whose fault is that? You kept me at arm's length the whole time we've gone out," he grumbled. "We weren't really dating, not in the physical sense." Tyler flushed angrily and fell silent.

"That's because it felt weird. We're only meant to be friends, Tyler. Please, let this go and move on. There's someone perfect out there for you if you'd just look," she waved an expansive arm and then pushed a tendril of hair away from her face. "It's really hot for June, isn't it?" It was a lame attempt to change the subject, but she was an optimist and smiled at him, praying he'd see reason.

She caught the distant sound of a jet and craned her

neck to find the source. The sky was a rich blue with a single fluffy cloud to mar the perfection of the hot June afternoon. A thin, white contrail streaked across the cerulean sky, like a line of glowing smoke that stretched out to infinity. Sunlight glinted off the plane's silver edges. Sarah found herself wishing she were up there already and winging her way to Italy where she planned to spend the summer teaching English at a school in La Spezia.

But she wasn't. She looked at Tyler's red face as they marched across the expansive grounds. It was a beautiful place for an early morning walk. Sarah had enjoyed the trees, flowers, and many footpaths as a child. A fountain, squatting at the center of the manicured lawn, gurgled with bubbling water as they drew close.

Leaping ahead to come alongside the water feature ahead of her, Tyler grabbed Sarah's arm. "I can't believe you're doing this to me," he said, his voice hard. Catching her other arm, he pulled her around to face him. "You're leaving for the whole summer, and I thought you'd be wearing my ring. Can you promise you won't find someone else while you're away, and that you'll give our relationship some serious thought?" He pulled her resisting body into his arms. "I'm in love with you."

"I don't plan on meeting anyone else, but I refuse to promise anything...I already told you, we're breaking up," she said, curling her hands into tight fists. "You and I are friends. I really think you should start dating. Find a nice girl while I'm away." She laid a consoling hand on his sleeve. "Anyway, there are things I want to do before I get married. For one thing, I need to get a job and work for a while."

"Are you insinuating I don't earn enough money for you?" Sneering, he waved an arm at the manicured grounds surrounding them. "I guess you're used to better."

"No. Don't be ridiculous. Your job has nothing to do with it." She took a deep breath. "I just want to find my own place in the world. After all, I didn't spend four years at university for nothing." She smiled at him consolingly. "You'll be fine. Now, let's get back to the house. I have to finish packing. Dad's driving me to the airport later this morning."

"I could have…"

"No," Sarah interjected before he could finish. "My dad's driving me and we're picking up Gemma on the way." Under the circumstances, she didn't want to submit herself for yet another embrace. Hastily she put distance between them, almost jogging back to the house. Tyler doggedly followed behind.

"I'll text you when we arrive, okay?" she said, climbing the steps to the elaborate patio and trying to sound upbeat. "Think about dating, Tyler. I want you to be happy. Bye," She threw open the back door and waved.

"Yeah. Bye," Tyler shoved his hands deep into his pockets and turned toward the driveway where he'd left his old pickup truck. Then, he turned back and shouted. "You think about what I said, too."

Sarah dashed inside the house breathing a sigh of relief. He'd been building up to this proposal for some time now, but she really didn't think he'd ask today. Maybe some time apart would help him to take stock of his life and realise this relationship wasn't what he wanted either.

Leaving for a couple of months was for the best. She'd just spent four long years in university to get her degree in education, paying her way through with summer jobs and tutoring on the side. Her parents agreed she should do something for herself before settling down to a full-time job teaching. So, when her best friend Gemma found the online advertisement, looking for people to teach English to adults for the summer, they'd both jumped at it. After having taken her only other holiday to France when she was nineteen, Sarah had always wanted to see Italy.

As she took the stairs two at a time to her bedroom, someone she'd met on that holiday floated into her mind, as he so often did. The memory of a man she had loved with all her heart—a darkly handsome Frenchman named Raphaël. But that was long ago, and she'd made a foolish, unalterable mistake, parting them forever. He was likely married with three kids by now.

Moonlight Over the Cinque Terre:
Chapter Two

"Of course, you should have come with me!" Gemma's face registered the shock she felt. "I can't believe you're still debating it. Everything's booked. We're going to have a great time, too."

Angling her head, Sarah gazed out the train windows. They rode the Cinque Terre Express carrying visitors and villagers to and from the idyllic villages of the area. Flashing out of tunnels and into the dazzling sunlight of a late August morning, it offered only a brief glimpse of the wonders that were yet to be seen and enjoyed in this beautiful part of the Italian Riviera. The Ligurian Sea, off to Sarah's left, danced beneath an azure sky as tiny pastel houses, clinging to the rugged coastline, beckoned.

"It's not so much debating the trip. No, it's more feeling guilty for splurging on myself rather than grabbing the next flight home. I'm already sitting on the train to Vernazza with you, so I can't very well turn back now." Sarah shrugged. "I just need assurance that it wasn't too selfish of me to take another few days before returning to Canada. I should be looking for a job." She sighed heavily.

"You have to put work out of your mind. It'll take care of itself." Gemma placed both hands on her knees and leaned toward Sarah with grim determination on her face. "You worked all summer, remember. Teaching English to a bunch of Italian business people wasn't a picnic. I thought it was pretty demanding, didn't you?"

"Yes, but…" Sarah sounded worried, even to her own ears. "I don't ever want to sponge off my parents. Now that university's behind me, I need to get my own place and start earning a living."

"You will. Gimme a break." Gemma rolled her eyes. "You're about the most responsible person I've ever known. Too responsible if you ask me. You have to live sometimes, you know. We're only twenty-four! We should be having fun."

As the train plunged into another tunnel, Sarah averted her eyes to the blue-flowered skirt she wore. Brushing lint from her knee, she considered what Gemma said.

She took a deep breath and grinned across the aisle at her best friend. "You're right. I'll lighten up and have a little fun."

"And does Tyler still write you?" Gemma's face tightened a little with her last words. She hadn't been in favor of her two best friends dating and lost no opportunity in telling them so.

Sarah sighed. "Yeah, he texts." She didn't want to discuss it. The subject had caused a few arguments between her and her friend. Sarah had only responded to Tyler's many texts once during the whole time she'd been away. And that was to tell him, yet again, to forget her and start living his life. She'd even told him she didn't want to be friends anymore. But from his messages after that, it didn't appear he was listening to anything she said.

Gemma sat back. Crossing her ankles, she put her hands behind her head as they emerged from another tunnel and turned her gaze toward the sea. She always dressed as though about to participate in a hiking expedition, and today was no exception. She wore longish khaki shorts, a pink tank top that bagged over her waistband, and clunky hiking boots with thick socks to protect her feet. Her customary ball cap had been pulled low over her eyes and large sunglasses completed the ensemble. A large backpack sat on the seat next to her and a cross-body purse, holding day to day items was slung at her side,

Gemma didn't fuss with makeup, preferring a fresh face. She left her dark brown eyes unadorned, although thick black lashes framed them nicely. Sometimes, she would smear a bit of clear gloss on her generous, smiling mouth. Though apart from that, she was as natural as she could be. Her hair was a glossy brown, the colour of roasted chestnuts, and fell to just above her shoulders. While her upturned nose was covered in freckles from all the time she spent outside.

"*Nessun problema*," she said, returning the grin once they were whisked into darkness once more. "See? I even learned some Italian while we were here. Anyway, that's what friends are for."

"What? For leading you on a wild getaway to the Cinque Terre?" Sarah laughed.

"Yes!" Gemma raised her voice with emphasis and then joined in the laughter.

Sarah's smile softened as they broke from the tunnel.

She peered through the window once again. "It's so beautiful here. I want to enjoy every moment. Once I'm working full-time, and maybe married someday, who knows when I'll be able to return to this wonderful place? Maybe never. Even a working holiday was tough to swing on my budget." She watched as Gemma began to apply sunscreen to her face and arms.

"Understood," Gemma spoke soothingly. "I know you're fiercely independent and wouldn't accept help from your parents, even though they could easily have paid for anything you wanted. Still…" she added, "I don't think you should hurry home. We've been in Italy, yes, but we haven't seen much of it. We should make the most our chance to explore while we're here."

She paused and a hint of laughter entered her voice once more. "Maybe, when we end this trip in Rome, you could look up the Pope and ask for a holiday blessing. Then you wouldn't need to feel guilty anymore." Laughing, she dodged the brochure Sarah threw at her and dropped the sunscreen into her bag.

Sarah felt better. Over the last few weeks, she'd emailed her resume to as many schools back home as she could find. Only she hadn't heard from any of them, yet. Teaching jobs were hard to unearth and the competition was stiff. However, she had confidence something would turn up.

"So, tell me about this B&B you booked for us?" Sarah settled back in her seat as they flew into yet another passageway. "You said it's supposed to have gorgeous views, right."

"It does. The Cinque Terre is fabulous from every angle, or so I've heard." Gemma picked up the crumpled brochure and waved it in the air before tossing it back. "Weren't you reading about Vernazza? Our B&B overlooks the village and has a panoramic vista. You're going to love it." She looked smug.

"Did you take that line straight from the pamphlet?" Sarah grinned at her then spoke again, with gusto. "I know I'll love it." A round arch of light had appeared ahead of the carriage. A moment later they burst from the tunnel under the mountain and into the intense light of midday.

As the train ground to a halt, Sarah glanced at her phone to check for messages. It was a reflex action. She hadn't expected to hear from anyone today, since it was only about seven in the morning on a Saturday, back home. Here, it was almost three in the afternoon. They really shouldn't have slept in. Most of the day was already gone.

The journey had only taken about thirty minutes to get to Vernazza from their boarding house in La Spezia. Why hadn't she made this trip before? She slid the device into her purse and slung the strap of the voluminous sack over her head to settle it at her side, straightening with anticipation.

The train had stopped three times already, to disgorge its passengers and take on more eager travellers. Gemma leapt up, following other passengers who rose to their feet and began shuffling toward the closest exit. Sarah waited for the throng of people to leave. Then, she reached into the overhead rack for her unwieldy bag, extended the handle, and dragged it down the aisle. She reached the steps, gingerly navigated them, jumped to the platform, and swung her bag behind her to skid across the cement.

Gemma waved to her over the heads of the many bodies all pushing for the exit and motioned that they would meet below the elevated station. She then set off, hoisting her backpack high on her shoulders, and tramping down the steps in her big boots.

Once on the street, Sarah spotted her friend at the edge of the rapidly dispersing crowd and made for her.

"First, we find the Azure Trail toward Corniglia," Gemma began in a loud imperious voice. "I think I see a sign for it over there." She pointed behind them to a high stone wall where an iron railing ran protectively along the top. At the spot where it joined the street there was a small plaque riveted to the rock.

"The B&B is a 600 metre walk. Up there," she waved a nonchalant arm toward the hillside as though it were just a quick jaunt around the block.

"What? Straight up?" Sarah almost gave herself a crick in her neck from looking up. She had expected a quaint little place in the middle of town, not some isolated dwelling suspended on the edge of an abyss.

It was pretty though. A jumble of colourful houses crouched along the lower portion of the mountainside, while rows of terraced vineyards ringed the rocky land almost to the top. The rollers of Sarah's case rumbled loudly across the pavement as she followed her friend toward the set of concrete stairs.

Sarah's heart sank. She could already see the foolishness of her attire, not to mention her luggage. Irritated with herself for lack of forethought, she now knew she shouldn't have worn a white blouse, flouncy skirt, and flimsy, high-heeled sandals. It was plain stupid. Of course, her friend could have given her a little warning.

As though knowing Sarah was thinking about her, Gemma shifted her backpack and stopped, turning to eye Sarah's hard-shell bag doubtfully. "Guess I should have told you it's all uphill and over rocky terrain." She made an apologetic face. "Oops."

"I'll manage. Thankfully, I only have to carry the thing

up once. It's my own fault." Sarah fluttered a careless hand, denying her inner dread of the climb. "Let's go."

"Alright. Call me if you need help." Gemma swung around to stride away. She was shorter than Sarah's curvy 5'6" frame, but was lean and fit from her time spent at her favorite pastime—hiking. Gemma loved a challenge and positively glowed with the prospect of a good ramble.

Grimly, Sarah lugged her suitcase up the steps and started pulling it along the cement sidewalk. So far, so good. She eyed the rocky landscape ahead as the trail became increasingly steep. Squinting against the blazing sun, she watched as her friend turned the corner and disappeared. So much for calling her if she needed help.

Holding her suitcase between her knees to prevent it from rolling away, Sarah paused to dig in her handbag for a hair elastic, sunglasses, and folded sun hat. The hat wasn't the most attractive article of clothing she owned, but it worked. She scraped her long hair into a low ponytail, stuffed the hat on her head, and slid the glasses into place. Then, puffing a little already, she braced herself for the walk. Judging by where Gemma had gestured, it was almost straight up the hillside. She didn't mind exerting herself, but this was ridiculous.

Having forgotten to bring sunblock, a major *faux pas* in this country, she scrutinised her bare arms and wondered how soon they and her face would burn in the hot August sun. She should have asked to borrow some cream from Gemma. But the girl was already too far ahead to call to, having broken into a stride fast enough to win some sort of endurance race. Sarah's complexion was as fair as the curly blonde hair that surrounded it and she noticed that her arms were reddening.

Lifting the case to carry it with both hands over a particularly rough patch of ground, she felt perspiration trickle between her shoulder blades. She thought back to the last time she'd been this hot. It had been in the south of France, on that same memorable holiday with her cousin Angelina, as they visited the Belliveau family. What a time they'd had. She'd brought too many foolish clothes on that excursion too. Sarah chuckled, remembering the memory happily, until she thought of Raphaël.

Despite all efforts to eradicate him from her brain, Raphaël's smiling face occasionally floated through her dreams at night. One couldn't control their dreams, after all.

As a culmination of the visit to Provence, Angelina had married the handsome Julien Belliveau, Raphaël's brother. Sarah hadn't seen her cousin for a long time. She'd even missed their wedding since university was just ramping up in Canada at that time. It was something she regretted bitterly.

Sarah came back to the present with a jolt as she stopped on the Azure Trail to catch her breath. Pushing a strand of waist-length, curly hair from where it had become stuck on her cheek, she used the hem of her blouse to mop her face. Not very lady-like, she realised, tucking it back into her waistband, but the end justified the means.

Despite her best efforts, Gemma was long gone. So, Sarah took a few moments longer to breathe. Moving to the side of the trail, she leaned heavily on a tree and panted. She'd lugged her bag up flight after flight of uneven steps chiselled into the stone and dragged it over rocks, roots, and rubble. Surely it couldn't be much farther. She lurched onward, hopeful.

Soon she came to a small wooden hut where a man sat fanning himself with a leaflet. He asked for her ticket to pass into the National Park. Producing it, she told him haltingly between puffs that she was lodging at a place called, The Point, just ahead. He waved her through.

Gazing at the grape vines that clung to the hillside above and below her, she passed through a small valley. Sarah knew the beautiful views she should be enjoying were hindered by her exhaustion and she felt sorry for it. The scenery was really gorgeous, but heat, thirst, and fatigue were all that consumed her now. She wished fervently for a drink of water. Hefting the suitcase, she now hated with a burning passion into her arms, she stumbled around a bend.

"Just keep putting one foot in front of the other," she said aloud. "You can do this." Then, suddenly she was overlooking the open sea. She stopped again, gaping in astonishment. The cliff fell away at her feet leaving her to feel as though she were dangling at the edge of the most beautiful precipice she had ever seen.

The sapphire waters of the Ligurian Sea sparkled in the sunlight, stretching to the horizon as far as she could see. A few clouds puffed across the sky, mirroring the deep blue waves that licked the rocky shores far below. Waves crashed over them in a white frothy spray. She heard the plaintive cry of seagulls and the endless chatter of cicadas in the trees behind her. Taking it all in, she pulled the fresh sea breeze into her lungs.

Her eyes glazed with tears. In the distance to her right, the scattered, colourful houses of Vernazza poked from the rock and native trees, extending to perch precariously along the promontory of solid, jagged stone that angled to the sea.

"Oh, it's too pretty to be true," she breathed. "I am *so* grateful to be here." Sarah lingered a moment longer and then, reluctantly she lifted the suitcase into her arms again and marched on. With a lifting of her heart, she saw a tiny white sign, tacked to the side of a rock, and knew she'd arrived.

"The Point," she murmured thankfully. Lifting the latch of a small wooden gate in need of paint, she left the path and looked up a narrow path where a large stone house hunkered above her in the pines and other assorted trees. The walkway was smoother now. Spiny cactus sprang from the rocky soil while potted plants filled with bright pink flowers and red geraniums lined her way. Overlooking the Ligurian Sea, to the west of the house there was a broad, raised patio with umbrellas shading several tables. Above it was a smaller terrace that Sarah assumed must serve the guest bedrooms.

Finally, she came to the platform leading to the entrance. It consisted of two, medieval-looking, wooden doors painted a bright glossy red and held in place by large metal fixtures. Lights hung from the stone wall on either side. Overtop, wisteria clung to the width of the dwelling, reaching to encircle the red-shuttered windows gracing the top level. As she stumbled up the flight of steps, decorated with an assortment of other bright flowers, Sarah wondered if one of those windows would be her room.

She set her suitcase down with a thump, extended the handle, and bumped it over the wooden slats to the slightly ajar door. Inside she could hear Gemma's voice. Hooray! She'd done it. Placing a hand against the heavy wood, she knocked, pulled it wide, and stepped tentatively into a large kitchen.

"*Benvenuto a casa nostra,*" a booming male voice called. As Sarah's eyes adjusted to the lack of light, a man leaped to attention, her shoulders were grasped, and she was drawn forward to receive three kisses that landed somewhere in the air next to her cheeks. She made out the hazy figures of the man and two others.

"*Ciao*," she replied with a smile. Standing her suitcase on its end, she included the man's wife in her greeting as the lady stepped forward with a similar welcome including a light kiss next to each of Sarah's cheeks. The couple looked young, perhaps in their early thirties. Somehow, she had expected older people to be running a bed and breakfast. The man was medium height with a shaved head and warm brown eyes in a tanned face that crinkled with smiles. He wore sandals, a floppy, short-sleeved blue button-up and a pair of brown shorts coming so far past his knees he looked like he was wearing regular pants that had shrunk, badly.

His wife was significantly shorter. She was plump and wore a sundress of bright purple that set off her dark hair and eyes. Her full red lips parted in an equally friendly grin.

"I am Romeo," the man said with a slight French accent, "and this is my wife, Luna. It is fitting do you not think so? Romeo and the moon…" He lifted his hand toward the ceiling as though the moon were visible at this very moment, then paused to wait for Sarah's response. She nodded in smiling agreement, having the impression he must ask every guest this very same question.

"It is so nice to meet you," she said. "I'm Sarah Peterson." She dragged a hand across her flushed face and took a breath before continuing. "I'm happy to be here."

"Please, come in and sit down," Luna said, resting a consoling hand on her arm. "You must be worn out."

Gemma joined them with a broad grin and Sarah couldn't help but feel a twinge of irritation with the girl. They'd lived in the same boarding house in La Spezia. Surely her friend should have told her to bring a backpack when she'd known full well they were staying halfway up a mountain.

Romeo lifted her suitcase in surprise. "You carried this up here? I am so sorry, *signorina*. That must have been terrible for you." He turned to consult with a fifth occupant of the room that Sarah hadn't noticed. A tall man stood in a wide arched entry at the far end of the kitchen, shrouded in shadow.

"Look what this girl carried!" Romeo hefted the case higher to show the man who appeared to move into the room with slow, deliberate steps.

Gemma jammed her elbow into Sarah's heaving ribcage and hissed in an undertone, "That guy is hot. Wonder if he's married?"

Sarah couldn't care less whether the guy was hot or not. She was sticky, puffing, and annoyed. But she plastered another smile on her reddened, panting face and held out an indifferent hand as the man walked toward her.

"So pleasant to see you again, Sarah," said a deep voice in a stiff French accent, taking her hand with only his fingertips.

Sarah knew that voice. It hit her like a thunderbolt from her past. Her head flew back and her mouth opened in a shriek.

"Raphaël!"

She felt her knees give out from under her and heard the sound of a chair scraping across the floor as someone rushed to grab her arm and help her sit down. She dropped onto it.

"W-what—what are you doing here?" She stared at him, her heart racing. Lifting a hand to push the hair from her eyes, she tried to focus. It was him, but she couldn't quite believe it. The room began to spin.

"Get this girl something to drink," Romeo barked.

But everything went dark as Raphaël's voice, as though reaching out from her dream world, said coldly. "I'd like to ask you the same thing."

Grab your copy...
vinci-books.com/moonlightoverthecinqueterre